ISBN: 978-0-9882927-0-3

Morningstar Ventures Inc.
P.O. Box 1723
Cave Creek, AZ 85327
Visit our websites www.MorningstarVentures.com
and www.EriksHope.com

Erik's Hope books are available at special discounts when
purchased in bulk for fund raising or other promotions. For
details contact us at the address above or send an e-mail to
contact@morningstarventures.com.

Printed in the United States of America
First Printing November, 2012
10 9 8 7 6 5 4 3 2 1

ERIK'S HOPE

THE LEASH THAT LED ME TO FREEDOM

FOREWORD

For most of her life, Andrea Chilcote prided herself on being pragmatic, goal driven and business savvy. She set her sights on the bottom line. She achieved success in the hotel industry and then launched a business coaching company. She projected outward strength and perfected the art of self-control, never letting her vulnerability peek out from her cloak of confidence.

Like her, I focused too much on acquiring professional achievements. I chased the almighty byline as a daily newspaper reporter and editor and rejoiced in scooping the competition. Being on life's sidelines and chronicling the fortunes and misfortunes of others seemed to be a safe place for me.

How many of us find ourselves consumed by

daily deadlines that we overlook the true simple joys in life? Like a dog begging us to play fetch? Or a cat wanting to purr in our lap?

In the peak of our careers, both of us took a leap of faith – and we can credit rescued dogs for giving us the confidence to feel fear, ask for help and yes, openly grieve. Thanks to Andrea's dog, Erik and my dog, Chipper, we are finally becoming truly human.

I left the W-9 world a dozen years ago to focus on my true passion: bringing out the best in people and pets. In my many roles as an author, animal behavior consultant and radio show host, not a day goes by that I don't learn something new from a dog or a cat. I've learned to listen to them. To watch them. They are wise teachers eager to enrich us spiritually and emotionally if we just push the pause button on our hurry-up world long enough to listen. Really listen.

And, I ask you to listen with your heart to Erik's Hope. This special book features powerful, compassion-filled dogs answering to the names of Erik, the Princess, White Wolf and more who shepherd Andrea through many key moments in life.

As you read, I hope you find yourself relating to the messages in this book as I did. Perhaps the words will stir up fond memories of your first pet or that special 'heart' dog who passed on far too soon. I hope

Andrea's words inspire you to never let fear replace your faith and to embrace that true friendship is eternal.

It's time for you to take a leap of spiritual faith. Call your dog or cat over as you read these pages and get ready to take a wonderful – and overdue – journey into the healing power of pets.

By Arden Moore
founder of FourLeggedLife.com

DEDICATION

To all animal welfare advocates whose tireless and sometimes thankless missions protect and elevate our sage four-legged teachers.

ERIK'S HOPE
THE LEASH THAT LED ME TO FREEDOM

PART I

· E R I K'S H O P E ·

IF THIS WAS ENOUGH

If this was enough, it would have ocean depths of joy and pain, intense feeling and numb nothingness, love, loss and simple friendship.

If this was enough, it would tell the story of how I thought I'd lost you forever, how I thought you were not real after all, just bones and blood and gristle destined to return to dust.

If this was enough, it would include the part about you coming back to me, precisely so, enough that even one as unconscious as I could detect the obvious.

If this was enough, it would tell of why we came together in the first place, what wounds you healed with tongue and fur and wolf song. It would tell of when we met each other's eyes and I knew that all would be revealed, all would work out, and that love is all there is.

If this was enough, it would talk of the sights and sounds, smells and tastes of unconditional love. Blazing orange sun over marshland, arid desert rocks stepping one by one, fur embraces and the smell – oh that smell – of warmth on fabric, alive with coursing pulses radiating like a soft hum.

If this was enough, it would include the days you went away literally or in your head, lost to us for minutes or excruciating hours wondering if you would ever return. It would talk of miracles and faith, moving mountains and finding out that John Lennon was right – all you need is love.

If this was enough, it would leave an indelible image of your face, white like sun bleached cloth, eyes deep syrup, a smile formed by your jawline. But no, that would not be enough. The reader would need to experience the awe of touching your coat, the pads of your paws, a whisker brush against skin. And still, that would not be enough.

The totality of the miracle, alpha to omega, beginning to never end, is all that is ever enough.

Andrea Chilcote

CHAPTER ONE

"I am doomed!"

The wolf-dog paced back and forth in the tiny cage, his overgrown nails clicking on the cement floor. Waiting, watching.

"Where is she?"

He listened anxiously for the kennel door to open and provide him with his only hope of survival since arriving at the Durango Street shelter. This place felt like jail for animals like him and other unfortunate lost or abandoned pets. Earlier, the wolf-dog had heard the people in charge say this was his last day. Now the sun was dropping below the level of the clouded block glass windows of the kennel and he knew his time was quickly running out.

His mind raced with questions. "Where can she

be? Doesn't she know I'm out of time? Doesn't she know I need her! Oh, please hurry!"

From deep in his heart came a strange feeling of certainty: "She must know she needs me! We have much to do together." And then the feeling quickly vanished.

The kennel door opened several times and each time the wolf-dog jumped to see if the woman had finally arrived. He heard one of the workers say it was almost three o'clock. He was getting really scared now. The wolf-dog had lived on the streets most of his life and there were many times just surviving had been a difficult task for him. The Arizona summers had been brutal, and there were occasions when he had gone several days without food. His situation now was different, and dire, but it wasn't because he was afraid of dying.

No, fear of death was not the issue. The wolf-dog was brave and wise beyond typical canine standards. He had a special sense that, for a long time, had beckoned to him, drawing him to his life's purpose. Though the feelings came to him intermittently and were brief, the wolf-dog was driven to find the woman. Somehow she was connected to his purpose. While he didn't fully understand why, the wolf-dog was most afraid of leaving this world with his mission incomplete.

It had all been arranged, though neither the wolf-dog nor the woman would completely understand their purpose in each other's lives for many, many years. They would enjoy a love that was thought of as uncommon between a human and a dog. While their greater mission together would slowly reveal itself, neither would fully realize it completely until the dog's inevitable death in the distant future.

Suddenly, a sound at the main kennel door! The wolf-dog leaped to the front of the cage and saw a woman come through the door. She looked and dressed differently than the shelter people. "Could it be her?" he wondered.

His body began to tremble with anticipation.

The woman walked down the aisle between the rows of cages where dogs barked and pleaded with her for freedom. The wolf-dog noticed she didn't slow her pace or look into their eyes. His instincts were pretty good and he knew she couldn't bear making eye contact with the other animals. If a dog could smile, he would have. He knew instantly why she avoided their eyes, and he liked her good heart.

The woman, whose name was Andrea, peered into his cage. He knew her immediately without a word being spoken.

"She's the one! Yes, she's the one! And she's finally here!" With uncontrolled excitement the wolf-dog began to twirl around in the small space making high yipping sounds. Happy paws drummed on the hard floor to the music of his own special song.

Andrea opened the door and looked straight into his eyes. No hesitation. There was an understanding without words. Andrea had come to save him.

Looking directly at him, she said hurriedly, "I'll be right back." There was such confidence in her voice; the wolf-dog had no reason to doubt her. As she walked away, her footsteps deliberate, he could hear her calling to the shelter workers, "I want him! I'll take him with me right now."

The wolf-dog listened intently to the verbal exchange between Andrea and the workers. He thought, "It's finally happening for me! She's here, this special person for whom I've been waiting so long." He vowed to become Andrea's best friend and companion. Little did he know that his commitment would last for all time. He sealed the bond by throwing back his head and giving her his sweetest howl, as if to say, "I've been waiting for you! Thank you for saving me!"

Andrea quickly completed the paperwork required by the shelter's adoption process and turned around to see one of the workers approaching with her new dog. A rough jute rope had been looped around his neck for a leash. The wolf-dog was straining against the rope, coughing and gasping for air, but that didn't matter. He didn't want to wait another second. He was ready to join Andrea and be free forever.

Andrea collected the makeshift leash in her hands and as her fingers encircled it, a feeling of peace and calm overcame her. It was the kind of feeling you get when you know all is well in your world. As she and the wolf-dog started for the door, a man in a white coat stopped them long enough to jab a needle into the dog's hip. The wolf dog let out a blood-curdling cry that pierced the ears of everyone within range. Andrea knew they were giving him required vaccinations, but she winced at his pain. Hurriedly, she pulled him toward the exit to remove them both from this terrible place.

Andrea had come to save the wolf-dog, and she too was compelled by some unexplainable purpose. She was absolutely driven and so determined to rescue the poor soul that she didn't even question his mangy wolf-like appearance or the horrid smell of his matted fur. Andrea saw through his outer appearance and recognized that he had a loving spirit and strong determination that drew her to him. What she didn't know was that this smelly creature with dirty fur hanging like dreadlocks from his skinny body would become her lifelong teacher, her companion and her very best friend. She also didn't know the meeting was one of providence rather than chance. It had all been arranged.

REFLECTIONS
Choices

Life is not a game of random chance. Nor is it a fatalistic series of predetermined events and outcomes. We show up here on earth with one purpose or many, all in service of growth in consciousness – our own and those whose paths we cross. Infinite potential is laid out before us, the players at the ready. The choices we make are largely dependent on our ability to look, listen and learn. Everything we need is available; it's a matter of tuning in.

Magic moments come along in every life. Sometimes these pivot points are disguised as mundane occurrences and other times they accompany trauma that seems pointless or tragic in the midst of its pain. At these choice points, we can shut down or awaken to the possibilities. There's neither judgment for holding back nor gold stars for opening up. There is a different kind of reward for heeding the whispers – the privilege to share the lessons in ways that pave a smoother path for others.

This is the story of one young woman's awakening to her purposeful path. What she learned with the guidance of her beloved dog enables her to help others transform their work, relationships, and lives.

CHAPTER TWO

On the weekend before the wolf-dog's last-minute rescue, Andrea and her husband Arthur had visited a woman who bred Samoyed dogs. Andrea and Arthur told Paula, the breeder, that they were interested in a puppy for Andrea. Arthur had a dog, the Princess, to whom he was quite attached, and Andrea wanted to enjoy the same companionship with a dog of her own.

After asking a lot of questions, Paula said, "It's obvious to me that the two of you love your Princess and would give another dog a very good home. But you are away at work too much of the day to properly raise a puppy."

She then told them about a veterinarian friend who took time each week to visit county facilities to alert her of dogs that were available for adoption. "There are over 50,000 homeless dogs that enter shelters each year in Maricopa County alone," she said.

"Why don't you rescue an adult dog that desperately needs a home?"

Andrea and Arthur were astounded at the number of homeless dogs and immediately decided they wanted to adopt one.

On the way home, Andrea said to Arthur, "It will probably be a long time before they find just the right dog for us."

While she knew that rescuing a homeless dog was the right thing to do, she couldn't help but feel a little disappointed.

"You might be surprised like I was," Arthur said with a twinkle in his eyes.

Andrea recalled how the Princess had come to them. She had been a gift from Andrea before the two had married. At the time, Andrea worked as a supervisor of the front desk at a hotel. One day, one of her employees came to work very distraught. Lucy, the desk clerk, told Andrea tearfully, "I don't know what to do. My husband hit our dog, Alice, with a broom this morning because she had trampled his petunias. He told me that he would kill her if she stepped in his flower bed again. I have to find her a safe home – now!"

Lucy showed Andrea a picture of a petite, snowy white Samoyed with large brown eyes. Alice was stunning.

At that time, Andrea had known Arthur for only a few months. Already she had learned he was a loving man who cared for animals. Just the evening before Lucy approached her, Arthur had told Andrea about the Irish Setter named Brownie whom he had befriended while growing up. Sadly, he had not had a dog since then, and he said he would like to have that companionship again.

Immediately upon hearing Lucy's story, Andrea thought, "Arthur, you're about to get your wish!"

She called Arthur and he agreed to meet Alice on the condition that he didn't have to keep her if he didn't like her. Andrea smiled and thought to herself, "You'll like her. Just wait until you see her!"

•

That same day, arrangements were made for Andrea to pick up Alice from Lucy's home after work. Arthur had insisted that Andrea make it clear to Lucy that this was a twenty-four-hour trial only – there were no guarantees.

When Andrea and Alice entered Arthur's apartment, he was sitting on the sofa. Andrea dropped the leash and Alice ran to Arthur, jumped onto the sofa, and smothered him with kisses. Arthur looked up at Andrea and barely paused before saying, "Call Lucy and tell her we're keeping the dog. Oh ... and I'll be calling her the Princess, because that's what she is."

REFLECTIONS
Synchronicities

Synchronicities are events that seem oddly related yet have no explainable or obvious causal relationship.

While Andrea did not consciously recognize it as such, Arthur's recollection of Brownie the night before Lucy appealed to her for help was a synchronous event. It set in motion a series of momentous opportunities.

Many people walk around in various degrees of numbness, perpetuated by the so-called stress of daily living. Few escape this fact of human life. Recently, when asked to share her sense of what was causing a particular issue, a colleague said, "My sense of it? I'm too frazzled to sense anything."

The signs and guideposts that point to a needed direction are there before us – shouting sometimes – and we often miss them in our busy-ness. Andrea could have missed or ignored the opportunity to adopt the Princess. Life would have gone on, likely with another catalyst presenting itself in the near future. Fortunately for this one dog in need, she heeded the message and was rewarded a thousand-fold.

Consider a coincidence you experienced – one that was mundane or transformational – it does not matter. What got your attention? What did you tell yourself about the event or situation, at that time or later? If you acted, was it a logical response or an act of faith sparked by intuition? Finally, what did this synchronicity yield for you or those around you?

"A coincidence is God's way of
remaining anonymous."

Albert Einstein

CHAPTER THREE

On Monday morning, the day after the visit with Paula the breeder, Andrea received a phone call. It was Paula's veterinarian friend. He said, "Andrea, I understand you and your husband would like to adopt another dog to become a companion to the Princess. Well, there's a young Samoyed dog at an overcrowded shelter who will not be allowed to live beyond this very day if no one comes to save him."

Heart pounding and mind racing, Andrea explained the situation to her boss, Pete. He graciously allowed her to leave work early to try to help the animal. Pete reminded her she still had several projects on her desk to complete before the end of the day, and she assured him she would return as quickly as possible and work as late as needed. Filled with determination, she rushed to the shelter to rescue the dog.

Now, leaving the shelter with the adoption behind her, Andrea looked down and began talking to the wolf-dog as if he were human. He had never experienced this before! She explained she had to go back to her office and finish a project for a client. "Then," she said, "we'll go home to meet Arthur, my husband, and our other dog, the Princess."

The wolf-dog jumped into the car as if he had been chauffeured around all his life. He sighed happily as Andrea removed the uncomfortable makeshift leash, then listened intently as Andrea drove and told him the story about rushing to save his life. Sitting right next to her in the front passenger seat, he kept one paw on her shoulder, as if to pledge his loyalty and offer his thanks. He held his head high.

"I know she loves me already," he thought to himself.

Once, at a red light, he looked down at his fur coat. As a puppy, his coat had been snowy white and fluffy, but it was now the brown-red color of Mississippi mud. He realized that he smelled bad too.

"I guess she must be blind to be able to see through to the real me," he thought. "That's great, because I like me the way I am. This is just too good to be true! Yippee!"

•

After a few miles of honking horns and stop-and-go traffic, the wolf-dog and his new friend arrived at her office. Before getting out of the car, she carefully slipped the rope-leash around his neck once again. "I don't need a leash!" he thought, but Andrea obviously thought differently. Obediently, he walked with her from the car into the building. Little did Andrea know how much her new dog would test her over the next few hours.

Andrea entered her office with the wolf-dog beside her. Immediately, he felt nervous. "I've never been in a building like this before. What are those strange smells? What is that whirring sound coming from that big machine? I've heard people talking about phones – could that be what those ringing sounds are? What kind of place is this?"

The room they entered had no windows, and everywhere he looked there were machines that made funny noises. People were moving about, but no one was smiling, nor did anyone stop to pet him. They gave him curious looks. Andrea seemed relaxed, but the wolf-dog was not. "This is no place for dogs," he thought. "I just want to have some fun!"

At her desk, Andrea tied the wolf-dog's leash to a nearby support pole and told him, "Be a good boy. I'll be right back."

Sitting tethered to the pole made the wolf-dog even more nervous and impatient. He watched his new friend moving around the office carrying papers and talking to a man she called Pete, her boss. He was the one who had been kind enough to allow Andrea to leave work for the rescue mission. Pete was friendly, but now that she was back from her rescue mission, he wanted her time and attention. The wolf-dog wanted it too.

Time passed. Andrea continued to be absorbed in the papers on her desk and occasionally in conversations with others in the office. The wolf-dog wanted her attention and the only way he knew to get it was to do something fun. No one had ever taught him that fun has its place and that inappropriate behavior might get bad results.

"I bet if I peed on this pole I could get her to pay attention to me and play!" the dog thought. So he did what wolf-dogs with few manners do – he lifted his leg and made a huge puddle on the floor.

"That should do it," he thought.

Andrea saw this out of the corner of her eye. Her mouth dropped open when she realized what he was doing. She moved so quickly that the breeze she created made her papers fly off the desk. She came running to find the carpet soaked, the warm liquid spreading further as she watched. The wolf-dog was proud and thought his tactic had been successful. She did rush to him – but then her boss came over and saw the damage as well! Pete had seemed nice enough before, but now he had a scowl on his face and spoke in a low voice to Andrea.

"Uh-oh. Pete's unhappy and it's my fault. I didn't know I would get Andrea in trouble. I just want her to play with me," the wolf-dog thought.

Realizing his mistake, he dipped his head sheepishly to his chest. He didn't want to disappoint the woman who had saved his life. He should have had more patience. "I'll have to work on 'being a good boy,' whatever that means."

Amazingly Pete just walked away shaking his head. The wolf-dog watched curiously as Andrea ran down a hall and came back with paper towels. She blotted the huge wet spot with towels, which began to absorb the moisture. He breathed a little easier about the mess he had made as he saw the damage disappear. She then bent down and hugged him and told him it was okay. "Just a little while longer," she promised, and she went back to her desk to try to finish as quickly as she could.

But it didn't seem like a little while. It felt like forever! He tried to be patient and lie quietly. He squirmed. He circled. He lay down. He got up. He howled gently – though she gave him a scolding look when he did that, so he tried very hard to stay quiet. "Being a good boy is hard work," he thought.

Just when the wolf-dog was doing his best work ever at patience, a man wearing a brown uniform entered the large office area. An alarm went off in his head – the wolf-dog recognized the uniform immediately.

The wolf-dog had a memory of a man in a brown uniform from many months before when he was running free on the streets. That man had chased him with a large net, wanting to capture him and put him in a truck with other barking dogs. The wolf-dog had run for his life to escape what he later learned was the "dog catcher."

On that frightening day, the dog catcher had chased him down a sidewalk and across several yards. The wolf-dog made a game out of the chase in the beginning, until he grew tired and the man started gaining on him. Then all of a sudden, he spotted one of his street friends up ahead in an alleyway. He raced forward as the friend signaled with loud barks for the wolf-dog to follow him, and they both ran as hard and as fast as they could along the fenced walls of the alley. They could hear the pounding of the dog catcher's boots on the pavement behind them. The man yelled and swung his net. He was fast, but not fast enough!

Within a few seconds, the wolf-dog's mangy friend led him through a small opening in the fence which had been hidden by garbage cans. As they escaped to the other side, they heard the dog catcher yell out, frustrated, "I'll get you sooner or later, you useless animals! You just wait!"

If dogs could "high five," the two of them would have raised paws to each other to celebrate their clever escape. But despite the victory, from that day forward, the wolf-dog was afraid of the brown uniform.

Now, at the office, as the uniformed man approached Andrea's desk with a package, the wolf-dog thought, "Andrea saved me – now I've got to save her from this man!"

He growled at the man, curling his lips and showing his sharp teeth. The ridge of hair along his backbone stood straight up from his body from his neck all the way to his tail. He pulled against the rope leash so hard that it choked his neck and made it hard to breathe. No matter how hard he tried, it wouldn't come off. He needed to protect this woman who had saved him. He had made a promise to her! He had to get free of the rope!

Unlike the dog-catcher, the uniformed man was clearly frightened. Andrea quickly signed the package acceptance forms as the man shoved the UPS parcel into her hands. He slowly backed away from the desk, then turned and ran out of the office to the safety of his delivery truck.

The wolf-dog felt his efforts were successful. "Ha, he won't bother us again! We're safe."

Just as the man in the brown uniform left the office, Andrea's boss came running over, again, to see the source of the commotion. He looked down at the wolf-dog. Pete's face was bright red and the look in his eyes was one of contempt.

"Oh, man!" The wolf-dog could tell this time Pete was really upset. He heard him tell Andrea that she should leave for the day.

"And take that dog, or whatever it is, with you," he said firmly.

Andrea apologized to Pete and decided the best thing to do was get out of there before anything else happened. She struggled with the rope to release it from the pole. The wolf-dog's straining against it had caused it to become so tight that it was almost impossible to untie the knot she had made earlier. Finally, freeing the leash, she grabbed her purse and said, "Let's get out of here." They quickly left the building and headed for the car.

As they settled in for the ride home, the wolf-dog thought, "I've already gotten Andrea in trouble twice and we haven't even made it home yet." What was in store for him next?

He looked over at Andrea with questioning eyes. She seemed to understand the quizzical look and said, "Don't worry, my beautiful friend, we'll be home soon. Arthur and the Princess are going to love you just as much as I do. You'll see."

He thought, "Wow, she called me 'beautiful.'"

The wolf-dog had never experienced this before. It felt good. He sat quietly and enjoyed the ride. But he couldn't keep from thinking about what the Princess would be like. He hoped they would be friends.

Soon all this thinking made the wolf-dog tired. He curled up in the seat to rest during the long ride home. "Home . . . a real, forever home," he thought, as his eyelids became heavy. For the first time in his life, the wolf-dog was content.

Just before his eyes closed, the wolf-dog thought he heard a voice in his head. The presence came to him more as a feeling than an actual sound, and he sensed deep love. "You did very well this afternoon, my friend. The journey has begun." Then, he dozed to the sounds of the music coming from the car stereo.

REFLECTIONS
Heart Awakening

On the ride to the office, this mangy street dog sat in the front seat of Andrea's car, gazing at her intently. He seemed to anchor unconditional love with his paw placed firmly on her shoulder. While she might not have had words to describe it at the time, Andrea felt his love and let it in.

The drive was the beginning of a much larger journey. It was the journey of awakening her heart. For the next ten years, the experience of loving this being so intensely and so deeply opened Andrea's heart full throttle. When the heart is open, the joy of life can reach us – and it's only when it reaches us that we can spread it outward.

The lives we live, complete with the characters that show up and the scenes that unfold, are a projection of what we believe about ourselves. By helping Andrea to open her heart and receive the love that's there for all, over time Erik's work allowed Andrea to know and love herself despite her human imperfections.

Many years later, a wise mentor offered Andrea a simple but powerful tool. The tool was a question that would become a compass for her as she sorted decisions and desires, mundane and critical. "Do you love yourself in this experience?"

Ask yourself this same question. Do you love yourself in the experience of your life at this moment? Consider your deepest desire. Can you love yourself in that experience? If the answer is yes, declare it yours.

"To love yourself right now, just as you are,
is to give yourself heaven."

Alan Cohen

CHAPTER FOUR

The peaceful drive home from the office was just a short break from more adventure. As Andrea's car neared the house, the wolf-dog rose from his nap and looked out the window. "Yay! A neighborhood with kids and other animals! Yippee, I can't wait to explore!"

Andrea pulled into the driveway. The wolf-dog was overcome with excitement, leaping over the top of her and out of the car the moment she opened the door. The wolf-dog bounded away from the car, the rope leash trailing behind him, heading straight for the busy street.

Frightened, Andrea screamed, "Come back! Come back this minute!"

Without thinking, she chased after him as he raced into oncoming traffic. She was wild with fear, thinking she would lose her new friend. As she was just about to reach the dog, she heard a sickening sound. A car screeched to a halt, narrowly missing both of them. A man and his young daughter jumped out of the car. The wolf-dog stopped – curious – then ran to the little girl.

Andrea had watched the scene unfold in slow motion, with no idea of what the wolf-dog would do. She had seen him only a short time ago ferocious in his attempt to get at the man in the brown uniform. How would he behave with this child? She quickly closed the distance between them, but not before the wolf-dog began running circles around the little girl and yipping to her to join him in play.

Not knowing whether to be afraid of him or play with him, the little girl timidly reached out and stroked his fur. Soon he began to smother her with kisses and she squealed, not in fear but with delight. The father looked on with caution, ready at a moment's notice to rescue his daughter from the dog.

"This is much better," the wolf-dog thought. "Now that I'm free of that scary office, I can be myself. I sure do love kids! They like to play as much as I do."

Despite the dog's rambunctious behavior, Andrea

was able to grab the leash and hold the wolf-dog close to her. The little girl continued to pat his head and talk to him as Andrea turned to the father and apologized. Then, with the leash firmly in her hands, they slowly walked back toward the car.

The car's engine was still running, and now the radio blasted a vintage Simon and Garfunkel tune. "Groovy is not how I'm feeling right now," she thought, as she turned off the ignition.

"What have I gotten myself into? What have I taken on?" It was as if she had suddenly become the parent of an energetic toddler. This apparently unruly animal was now her responsibility, as if he were her child. He definitely had a lot of energy. She wondered to herself why she had been so driven to get this dog, as she realized he was going to be a handful.

Simultaneously, the wolf-dog thought about how Andrea was reacting to his playfulness; he knew he had to be more careful with her. "If she gets this upset over a little run, what would she do if I played the way I did on the streets?"

As they continued toward the house, the wolf-dog thought if he was going to enjoy his new home, he had to teach Andrea to have fun, too! And it was pretty obvious to him that she had much to learn about fun.

Andrea was still shaking and short of breath from the chase as she stepped onto the porch. Arthur was waiting at the front door, having heard the ruckus outside after Andrea's car had pulled into the driveway.

The wolf-dog's introduction to Arthur didn't go exactly as Andrea had planned.

Andrea proudly stepped forward to introduce her new friend to Arthur, who took one look at the dog and asked her, "What's that?" His tone was not kind.

Andrea's disappointed expression did not deter him. He continued, "Have you lost your mind? This is a skinny, dirty wolf-like animal – nothing like our Princess. What were you thinking? And that smell!"

A beautiful snowy white Samoyed, the Princess, stood nearby and seemed to turn up her nose in a show of support for Arthur. She agreed completely with his opinion of this – this smelly creature.

Clearly, Andrea had some convincing to do. By now, the wolf-dog had learned that she was defending him and that he should display his best manners – if only he had them. He stood by her side with his head cocked, listening to the dialogue between them.

Within the hour, Andrea somehow persuaded Arthur that underneath all the dirt and matted fur, there was a handsome, loving dog. She told him she had decided to name him Erik because he looked like a strong Viking from the cold north. Perhaps the fact that the wolf-dog now had a name softened Arthur, because he agreed to help give Erik his first real bath.

Erik wondered, "A bath? What's a bath?" In the spirit of getting along with everyone in his new home, he followed Andrea and Arthur down the hall to the bathroom.

The Princess followed curiously from a safe distance and thought, "This should be interesting. That smelly creature sure needs a bath."

Andrea began drawing warm water into the bathtub. Arthur collected the shampoo and towels normally used for the Princess.

"Okay, so far, so good," Erik thought.

Everything appeared to be going just fine until...

Arthur lifted the dog and moved toward the tub of water. When the realization hit Erik that they intended to put him – *him* – into the water, he panicked. Feet went everywhere. Claws grabbed anything on which they could get the leverage needed to help Erik pull himself out of the tub.

Arthur and Andrea tried to soothe him with their voices but Erik, never having had a bath before, was outraged despite their efforts to calm him. Water splashed everywhere! The walls, the floor and the people were soaked. Finally, so was Erik.

Erik pleaded with his howls, "Don't you realize how much worse the water makes me smell?" Whining and crying did absolutely no good. He was condemned to the soap suds.

The Princess watched from the doorway, looking smug. Slightly disgusted, she thought, "They'll never get that smell out of his fur. Surely they're not going to let him sleep with us."

Finally it was over, or so Erik thought. Andrea toweled him off and made a feeble attempt at trying to brush through his dreadlocks. There was no doubt in her mind that the fur had to be dried before going to bed or no one would get any sleep from the awful wet-dog smell. They took Erik downstairs to continue the drying with, of all things, a hair dryer. He didn't like the hair dryer any better than he had the water, but he did his best to put on a brave front. After all, he was trying to impress Arthur.

Before too long, Erik was dry enough. Andrea and Arthur stopped the blowing and combing. Erik was so happy to be out of the water and away from the blower that he began to bounce around on the floor. He actually coaxed the Princess into playing with him. Yes, playing with him. Andrea and Arthur looked on in amazement. They had not seen her romp around like this in years.

They also noticed that in the play, the Princess was clearly letting Erik know that she was the boss and the dominant dog in his new home. There was no doubt she would hold authority over him, and, while she would grow to love him, her alpha role would remain for as long as she lived.

Playtime ended. Erik sat quietly and listened as Andrea and Arthur cooed to the Princess.

"Princess, you will always be my most precious girl dog," said Arthur. "We've all had a very exciting day. Let's go to bed."

Erik watched in amazement as Arthur, Andrea, and the Princess climbed into their warm, soft bed.

"Imagine that!" Erik thought. Determined to be part of the family, Erik jumped up on the bed. He leaped to Andrea's side and snuggled up against her. Arthur complained about the fur smell – it was going to take more than one bath to get Erik clean – and he told Andrea, "Keep him on your side of the bed!"

The Princess sighed in agreement and curled her tail over her nose.

Andrea was happy to have Erik next to her. Exhausted from the rescue adventure and the bath, sleep was upon them soon. Arthur and the slightly perturbed Princess positioned themselves on one side of the bed, and Andrea and Erik settled on the other. At least for that night, all was right in the world.

CHAPTER FIVE

At breakfast the next morning, Andrea and Arthur discussed the coughing they had heard from Erik through the night. Andrea thought it was from the rope that had choked his neck several times on the previous day. But she had removed the rope leash immediately upon arriving home yesterday. What if it wasn't from the leash at all? "Perhaps," she worried out loud to Arthur, "it's some horrid disease he picked up living on the streets."

Andrea fixed her gaze on Erik. He was lying comfortably on the floor next to her, his head resting on one of her feet. She bent down to touch his back and felt a gentle jolt. It was as if Andrea's body and Erik's formed a loop of energy. For a split second they were one. At first Andrea was startled, then tears began to fall.

"Arthur, what if he dies?" Andrea knew at that moment she loved this creature and couldn't bear to lose him. She was reminded of the panic she'd felt the day before when Erik had bolted into traffic and was surprised by her own feelings. "How could a person become attached so quickly?" she wondered out loud. Then, she remembered Arthur's instant bond with the Princess and smiled.

Arthur thought Andrea was being a bit dramatic, but he tried to ease her worry by suggesting they take him to the veterinarian early that morning. And so they did.

At the vet's office, Erik found himself once again in a strange environment and he didn't like it. There were a number of other dogs and cats waiting with their owners. Some of the animals had shaved places on their bodies with bright pink scars. Others were very old and could barely stand. The cats in their little cages were especially unhappy with all the barking dogs. They meowed so loudly you would have thought there was a full moon in the sky. It was very unnerving to a street dog to be confined with a leash in a room with strange dogs and a bunch of noisy cats.

Soon they were called back to see the doctor. "Erik Chilcote?" a woman in a white coat asked.

"Oh, no! More people in white coats!" Erik remembered the sharp pain in his hip from the day before, when he and Andrea were leaving the shelter. He didn't like the looks of this.

Andrea began soothing Erik. She stroked his fur to try to calm him down. Even Arthur said, "Erik boy, it's okay. Everything will be all right." At least he had two people who loved him at his side when the doctor came in.

After examining Erik, the doctor reassured both Andrea and Arthur that Erik's cough was from his stay at the shelter. It was called "kennel cough." He explained, "Dogs can get kennel cough when they are confined close together with other animals that have not been properly inoculated and cared for." He told them that with love, good food and a little medicine, Erik would be just fine in no time. And he paused and looked at Andrea thoughtfully, then said, "That's a fine dog you've saved, underneath the matted fur."

Andrea smiled. She hoped Arthur had heard that!

Andrea and Arthur paid the bill, made their way back to the car, and soon they were out of there.

Much to Erik's dismay, the next stop was the groomer. Not just any groomer, but the Princess' groomer! Erik listened as Andrea and Arthur talked about how pretty he was going to be when the groomer finished with him. "Pretty?? That's a girl-dog word," thought Erik. He could see it now! He would come out of this dog spa with bows in his hair, smelling like perfume. He had seen dogs looking like this and now he had an idea of how they got that way.

"Ugh!" he snorted. Erik sure hoped none of his street friends were hanging out around the corner watching for cute girl dogs coming out of this beauty salon. Being discovered in this place would be disaster to his reputation. "How will I ever live that down?"

While worrying about how he might look if his friends caught a glimpse of him, he didn't even think about how he was going to get to look "pretty." But reality hit again as they entered the salon. "Another bath – that means more water! Water and soap suds, and that loud blower contraption!"

Erik gave Andrea pitiful pleading looks, but she just smiled and patted his head.

Soon, the lady called "the groomer" came into the waiting area to get him. She looked down, put her hands on her hips and said in an exasperated tone, "This will not be easy. Erik will need several visits to get this mess cleaned up." She added that she was making no promises.

Erik gave Andrea one last pleading look, knowing

it was hopeless. He was about to lose his street look and that was an insult. He had really enjoyed sleeping in the bed with his new family, but there had to be limits to what a street dog could bear, and smelling like a cream puff was not one of them. He started to bolt for the door, and then remembered that these loving people were trying to help him. He forced back a growl and gave a sigh of resignation – a sigh that would become his trademark any time he had to forfeit his own wishes to a human.

Erik lowered his head and moved toward Marge the groomer. She led him to what he viewed as torture: a sudsy bath.

To him, the bath was every bit as miserable as the one the night before. Worse perhaps, as this stern, committed woman had no sympathy for him. Her job was to get him clean and she went at him with a vengeance. Water first, then the perfumed smell of shampoo that street dogs detest.

Soon, Erik's body was consumed in bubbles and perfume. "Ugh! How could Andrea do this to me?" he wondered. He reminded himself again of the promise he had made the day before. "I'll do my best to be good. But it's looking like this is going to be a very hard promise to keep."

Marge would not let up. She scrubbed his fur

and skin over and over again. After the shampoo was rinsed out, Marge squirted something called conditioner on his coat and worked it all through his fur. Then more water.

Out of the corner of his eye, Erik caught sight of the dog on the next table. She was white and fluffy, with fur shaved close to the body in places. He heard someone call her a poodle. The poor dog's skin was pink! Pink! He feared that with all the scrubbing, washing and rinsing his skin would soon be pink, too, just like the poodle's. At the sight of the pink and white poodle, panic struck Erik, and he struggled to free himself of the groomer's hold. With his body still very wet and slippery with conditioner, he was able to slide from her hands. As soon as his feet hit the floor, he headed straight for the front door.

On her own turf, the clever groomer could out-maneuver this smart street dog and easily tackled him as he flew by. Freedom lasted only a few seconds. "Marge must have lots of experience with escapees," thought Erik. "She nailed me!"

Without missing a beat in her determined process, Marge lifted Erik back to the table and began again. Erik let out another sigh as he surrendered, and he endured the balance of the day without incident.

When Andrea and Arthur arrived to pick him up

late that afternoon, Erik was almost unrecognizable. His fur was whiter and softer and he smelled wonderful. Andrea threw her arms around his neck and immediately began telling him what a beautiful prince he had become, while smothering him with kisses. "Well, maybe it was worth it after all," he thought.

Erik realized how tired he was as he jumped up into the car. He was soon making circles to nap for the ride home. As he dozed off, he briefly thought about home and hoped the Princess would not make fun of his girly smell. She would have something to say, that was certain.

Just as sleep had nearly come, Erik felt the loving energy that he had experienced the prior day.

"Who are you?" Erik asked.

"Some think of me as a guardian angel. Others call me a guide because I help them find direction. I am really just a part of you; in fact, I'm a part of All That Is."

"I hear you, but I can't see you. What do you look like?" Erik asked.

The response came just as Erik surrendered to sleep. "Anything you can imagine."

For now, sleep felt good.

REFLECTIONS
Empathy

Some years ago, an animal rescue organization printed t-shirts with the phrase "We're responsible for what we tame."

While it's necessary to put domestic animals through the rigors of veterinarians and groomers to keep them safe and healthy and to make it possible to share our homes (and even our beds!), they often have tremendous fear of these things we take for granted.

Erik was a gentle, loving companion, and at the same time there was always something wild about him. Andrea had the sense – especially in the later years – that he had graciously and selflessly agreed to forfeit his freedom for his role in her life. Much of that role was, quite simply, to allow himself to be cared for.

The animals are our teachers, part of the collective soul or consciousness that makes up All That Is. While they are wise beyond human comprehension, they are equally dependent upon our compassion and care. For Andrea, the simple act of caring for Erik's needs awakened in her a fundamental human quality – empathy.

Prior to adopting Erik, Andrea had gone about her life with detached responsibility. She had met challenges and solved problems with an exacting, objective approach, unencumbered by emotion. In college she had mastered difficult courses of study in math and science and she'd considered herself a scientist at the core.

The unexplainable feelings and instant bond Andrea experienced with Erik in the early days were a linchpin for the skills she would need to do her ultimate work. Our feelings – emotions – are the conduit for empathy. While often being tagged as "touchy-feely," empathy is really the doorway through which one human enters another's experience. It's through this passageway that we build intimacy and authenticity in relationships, and influence outcomes in positive ways.

"Empathy is a means of understanding other human beings," says Daniel Pink, author of *A Whole New Mind*. "Empathy makes us human. Empathy brings joy. Empathy is an essential part of living a life of meaning."

Through high school and into college, Andrea

had thought she wanted to be a doctor. Looking back, she was motivated by a universal desire to heal and help, but she was naïve in thinking that medicine was simply a science of formulas that, when applied based on research and rules, worked predictably. An early experience, the illness and subsequent death of her father, changed that belief.

Andrea's dad was diagnosed with leukemia about the time she entered college. At that time in medical history, science was not sufficient to save him. But this was not all that gnawed at Andrea. She had experienced the trial-and-error nature of her father's various treatments, and this new form of responsibility frightened her. She was beginning to understand that many things in life require faith and best judgment, and that was terrifying to the detached scientist.

The observation became more stark during an internship she completed during her senior year of college. Andrea had the privilege to spend a month with a well-respected emergency room physician. She literally shared his life, observing trauma situations, attending board meetings, and dining with his family. This experience only solidified her fears. This doctor had the gift of being a brilliant scientist while showing great empathy for his patients. Andrea saw that even with his sharp intellect, his extensive training and his uncommon compassion, he could not heal everyone. She saw him make mistakes and that was not something her scientific mind could accept. She could not take an oath to "do no harm" – what if she did?

Years later, full circle, Andrea's work is, at its core, healing work. Without having had the experience of opening emotionally to her own feelings as well as those of others, she would not have access to the channel called empathy, a channel that is a primary tool for taking appropriate responsibility. Without a shared perspective, we operate as islands, when in reality we are all connected. With empathy as a catalyst, we can change the world.

Ironically, what Andrea saw as responsibility in her early years was actually fear of making a mistake. Responsibility requires that we step out, fully engaging logic and intellect, emotion and intuition, and that we take risks. True empathy, not sympathy, is a compelling call to action.

Do you ever close your eyes and ears, literally or figuratively, to block intense feelings? What are the triggers? What might you be missing?

CHAPTER SIX

As time went on, Andrea and Arthur became absorbed in their work; they spent long hours away from home and were exhausted each night. They missed quality time with each other and with their special dogs.

To make it easier on Erik and the Princess during those long work days, Arthur installed a doggy door. The door allowed the dogs to visit the grassy fenced patio in the backyard of their house as often as they wished. But Erik wanted human companionship, not just the convenience of a door.

Erik pondered, "Andrea and Arthur are always working so late. I need to find a way to let them know how unhappy I am. What can I do to make them understand that I want more time with them?"

Erik shared his plan of action with the Princess.

After listening, she responded by saying, "Are you out of your mind? If you pull a stunt like that you're going to make them angry, not happy to spend time with you! Think about it, Erik. Doing what you're suggesting isn't the solution. I want more time with them, too, but I refuse to participate with you in this kind of behavior."

Erik thought about what the Princess had said. She was a good teacher and was usually right about things, so he delayed any action for now. But it was just a matter of time before his need for play and attention would surface again.

One day when Andrea and Arthur were working very late again, Erik couldn't control his frustration any longer. He didn't consult with the Princess this time. "I know she'll try to talk me out of it," thought Erik, "so I'm just going to do it!"

Erik waited until the Princess was taking her afternoon nap, then he quietly walked over to the back door and did the unthinkable. He pooped just inside the doggy door, on the carpet. Satisfied that this would finally get his family's attention and cause them to understand how much he needed to run and play, he thought, "They're going to step in this on their way through the door. Tomorrow, they'll think about the bad smell and will remember to come home earlier."

But Erik's ploy backfired. He only infuriated Arthur and Andrea, just like the Princess had warned.

Discovering that pooping by the door didn't bring them home earlier, Erik tried a new trick. He destroyed the blinds covering the front door by chewing them off as high as he could reach. At least now he could watch for them all afternoon and see them pulling into the driveway. While Erik thought that half-eaten blinds were a funny sight, Andrea and Arthur didn't think so and began losing patience with his antics.

They both understood that Erik was doing bad things to get their attention, but they didn't know what to do. What a dilemma they had!

With Erik now in their lives, Andrea and Arthur had plenty of fodder for mealtime discussions. Finding a solution to the daily doggy surprises was of paramount importance.

After much discussion, they decided to move closer to their offices so they could get home earlier each day and spend time with the dogs.

And so they moved to a new home in Chandler, Arizona, just minutes from their work. Little did they know the mischief would not end.

CHAPTER SEVEN

It was the day of the move, and boxes were everywhere in the new house. Andrea and Arthur decided to let the dogs explore their new fenced backyard while they got the house in order.

Erik was excited and raced around the yard like a mad dog. "What fun to be able to play without a leash!" He made encouraging yipping sounds to the Princess to get her to join in his fun, and she did for a while. He was glad he was able to convince her to loosen up and play; she needed to learn how to be a dog and have fun!

The summer heat of Arizona seemed to bother the Princess more than it did Erik – most likely because she had been raised in air conditioning and he'd spent most of his life outside. After a brief play time, the Princess reported, "I'm just going in for a while and take a short nap." And in a motherly tone, she warned, "Don't do anything foolish."

"Sleep is just way too boring," thought Erik. "What this new home needs is some excitement." Now alone in his new backyard, Erik began scoping out the place looking for adventure, and it didn't take long.

As he explored every nook and cranny, he slipped into his wolf-dog state of mind, looking for a little action. He prowled along the borders of the fence, searching for an escape route. Erik was proud of the Houdini tricks he had learned from his street friends. Andrea and Arthur had no clue how clever he really was.

He sniffed along the stucco covered walls that created the boundary for the yard. He examined little holes where animals had burrowed. The animals must have known he was coming because they were nowhere to be found. "Nothing of interest here," he thought.

There were several open spaces in the wall where iron fencing had been used instead of stucco. Erik could see an exciting world out there beyond the boundary. It was just too tempting and he began testing every rung of the fence, pushing them with his long, sturdy nose. At last, one moved. Freedom!

"Oh boy, time to take a little run!" Erik pushed his body through the space created by the rusted rung and bolted.

A quick thought crossed Erik's mind as he raced away from his new home. "I know this is against the rules, but I just gotta do it!" The Princess' warning was forgotten – old habits are hard to break.

Meanwhile, still in the house opening boxes, Andrea had a funny feeling that something was wrong. She decided to check on Erik and after frantically calling for him, discovered he was missing from the yard.

"Oh, no! How could he have gotten out?" she thought. "All the gates were closed and locked!" She screamed for Arthur to come help her find him.

Andrea was really worried. Not only was Erik unfamiliar with their new neighborhood, but there was a busy freeway nearby. She and Arthur ran up and down the sidewalks looking for him and calling his name. Their new neighbors peered out windows wondering what the fuss was all about. They saw two frantic strangers searching for someone they supposed was a child named Erik.

With so much to discover close by, Erik didn't have to go very far to find adventure. He couldn't wait to tell the Princess about his exciting exploration.

"There are all kinds of animals here in our new neighborhood! Rabbits are burrowing in the yard two houses over, and there's a cat outside. Imagine that? A cat! He must be pretty smart to avoid those sneaky coyotes," Erik thought.

But his excitement was interrupted. Andrea found him checking out the neighborhood, and soon Arthur caught up and joined her. Instead of sharing in his fun, they were shouting angry phrases Erik couldn't understand, like "dangerous freeway." He understood the phrase "bad dog," but didn't know what the big deal was. He was just exploring!

After the scolding stopped, Andrea hugged him and told him how worried she had been. Erik liked the hugs and kisses – but secretly couldn't wait until he was left in the yard and could escape again. This was the most fun he had had since leaving the streets, and he just had to go do it again! His chance would come soon.

Once home, Andrea inspected all of the gates to make sure they were securely locked. She found nothing to indicate how Erik had escaped. She said to Arthur, "One of us must have left the side garage door unlatched – it's the only way he could have escaped."

Arthur knew she really meant that he must have left the door open. But he shrugged off the accusation and promised to be careful. The dogs were allowed out again and Andrea went back to unpacking boxes.

The Princess marched up to Erik. She knew what he was thinking. "I know what you did, and why you did it, Erik. I know your instinct is to roam free, but you left the shelter and made the decision to be a part of this family. You must settle down and follow the rules. Don't do what I know you want to do again. You'll be in big trouble, Erik. And you could get yourself killed."

And the lecture didn't stop – she just kept on, "You know Andrea and Arthur are too busy to go chasing around the neighborhood looking for you. Just try to be good. Okay? Remember, the move to this new house was for us, and this yard is so much nicer than where we lived before. Don't make them worry again."

Erik looked back at her and was sure he saw a tiara sitting on her head, gleaming in the Arizona sun. "Miss Goody Four Paws!" he thought.

Deep down, Erik knew the Princess was right about his need to roam. The Samoyed breed is nomadic. This means they don't like to stay in one place for very long. It's a very big part of who they are; it's in their DNA.

Erik was a street-wise dog. He had been on

the streets for a long time before the animal control officers had picked him up. He liked to explore and just walking around in the fenced area wasn't much fun without someone to play with. The Princess was in one of her moods and was no fun at all. Her scolding didn't deter Erik. For a few seconds he struggled with the pull for wanderlust and his commitment to be a good companion to Andrea. He was on a roll, and once again, his instincts won.

"Time for another run!" he said to himself. He touched his nose to the rusty rung and off he went – again! This time he expanded his territory, wandering far beyond what was safe.

Erik quickly checked out the rest of his neighborhood to get his bearings and soon made his way over to a wide street with cars speeding by. "I think this is the busy freeway they were talking about. It must be lots of fun, judging by their excitement earlier. I'll just walk along beside the road and see where it goes," he told himself.

Cars zoomed by as Erik trotted along. They were going much faster than on the neighborhood streets. It was a little scary but as long as he stayed on the grassy shoulder, he felt safe. He walked for a long time, sniffing the smells of the highway and experiencing the rush of vehicles close by. A car slowed and pulled off the road behind him. As he turned to see what was going on, a man called out to him. "Hop in," he said.

"He looks like a nice guy. I'll catch a ride with him. Maybe he'll take me back home to Andrea and Arthur." Without hesitation, Erik jumped right into the car.

The man drove a long way before he finally slowed and entered a neighborhood. Erik was confused. The man was nice enough to give him a ride. "But this doesn't look like home," he thought.

"Oh well," he thought. "Adventure time!"

A short time passed, and the car stopped in front of a large house. The man fiddled with Erik's collar, opened the car door and walked him through the house out to the backyard. There was another dog just like him! "Oh this will be fun. Let's play!" said Erik. He romped with his new friend as if they had been playmates forever.

Erik was unaware of the panic Andrea and Arthur were experiencing. Little did he know they were now running up and down the streets and sidewalks, frantically searching for him. Exhausted, Andrea asked Arthur to continue to walk through the neighborhood while she went home to see if Erik had returned.

Pacing the floor and wringing her hands, Andrea

was crazy with worry. Then, the phone rang. "How strange," Andrea thought. "Who would even have our new number yet?" She had forgotten that the first thing she had done upon entering their new home was to put updated identification tags on both dogs' collars.

In a neighborhood far away, Erik was getting tired, and once again, a little bored with fenced play. He heard a car pull into the driveway of the man's house and seconds later he heard the doorbell ring. Shortly afterwards, he was led into the man's living room. There stood Andrea and Arthur with very worried looks on their faces. Erik looked up, "Oh wow! Look who's here!"

"Uh-oh! Andrea's not smiling. Arthur's not even looking at me. I'm in trouble!"

Erik tucked his head and tail ever so slightly and listened. He learned that Andrea and Arthur had received a phone call from the man and then had driven a very long way to get to the man's home. On the phone, the man had assured them that Erik was safe and playing in his backyard with his own Samoyed.

He said, "I found your dog walking along Interstate 10 and was worried that he would be hit by a car. So, I picked him up and brought him home. I almost didn't call the number on Erik's collar because I liked him so much, and I really want a playmate for my dog."

The man continued, "But, I want to do the right thing, and because he looked well cared for, I knew he must have a loving family who would miss him."

Arthur and Andrea thanked the man and Erik heard them offer to pay a reward. The man refused their offer and wished them well. With the leash securely fastened to his collar, Erik sheepishly followed Arthur and Andrea to their car.

On the drive home, Andrea sat in the back seat with Erik. She stroked his fur, buried her head in his neck and whispered into his ear. She told him she loved him and said she was scared that he might have been lost or hurt.

He lay down on the seat beside her and thought, "This must be what unconditional love is all about. She's had to come find me twice today – both times with a worried look on her face. But, when she gets to me she holds me and hugs me and kisses my face. She tells me how afraid she is that she might lose me. Even though I know I've made her unhappy and I've gone exploring without her, she still loves me."

"Wow. This kind of love feels really good! I'm beginning to think I'm a pretty lucky boy." Erik snuggled his head onto Andrea's lap and began drifting off to sleep.

It had been several months since Erik had joined the family. Often, just before going to sleep, Erik would sense immense love. It was the same sensation that he had felt so strongly in the car the first two days following his rescue.

Erik imagined the presence as a kind and gentle animal. It resembled him, except that it was much larger – three or four times his size. It was covered with long white fur like his and had light brown liquid eyes that seemed to reflect images like a mirror. Its mane was much more full and longer than that of any Samoyed. In fact, the mane was as full as a white lion's, though its face was decidedly wolf-like. Erik called the being "White Wolf."

As if Erik's thinking about White Wolf was a signal for him to appear, suddenly he did! Erik was surprised and thought he could almost reach out through his imagination and touch the soft fur.

"Erik," White Wolf began, "do you ever doubt the great love that Andrea feels for you?"

"Well . . . when I do bad things like running away, I'm surprised that she forgives me – even though she says she is happy to have me back." Erik replied.

"Never, never doubt her love for you. It is as

strong as yours is for her. This will be an important part of the work you will do together."

"Work? White Wolf, what do you mean?"

"You will understand in time, Erik." White Wolf faded away as Erik drifted deeper into sleep.

Andrea looked down at Erik and thought she could almost feel his love. She thought about how lucky she was to have found him. She also thought about the great responsibility of having an animal companion. She didn't want to lose him again and was anxious to find Erik's escape route in their new backyard.

•

Once home, Andrea and Arthur had one mission – to find the escape route. Like detectives, they planned the mission. Arthur said, "I'll go hide just outside the fence where Erik can't see me and you watch from the window. If he's getting out through the fence itself, we'll know it immediately."

Andrea let Erik out the door, and she and the Princess dashed to a window to watch. The Princess knew exactly what would happen next. It didn't take long.

Andrea gasped, "Oh my goodness! Look at him –

what a smart dog!" Erik walked to the iron fence and pushed the rung aside as if it were a flimsy rope. "So that's how he escapes!" she exclaimed. She raced out the door shouting, "Arthur, run quickly to the iron fence in the wall. That's where he's escaping. Hurry, hurry!"

Arthur moved immediately around to the back of the fence and raced toward Erik. He managed, just barely, to catch hold of him. "Gotcha big boy!" said Arthur. Erik's escape trick was foiled.

Meanwhile, if dogs could roll their eyes, the Princess would have. She thought, "I could have told them about that foolish dog's prank – if only they had asked me. Having Erik in this family has certainly livened things up. Erik should have listened to me when I told him not to do it again."

There was no way Erik was going to be allowed in the backyard again without a leash until the fence was repaired. A quick phone call was made to the repair man and by the next morning, the fence was secure. As she reflected on the events of this very busy day, Andrea pondered, "What will my smart friend think of next?"

CHAPTER EIGHT

Andrea continued to spend long hours at work. She was a sales manager, pre-opening a new hotel, the Phoenix Airport Hilton. As the grand opening neared, activities increased and so did the stress. Moving closer to work had seemed like a great way to increase time spent with her family but it required the discipline to leave the office; something Andrea had not yet mastered.

Erik listened each evening as Andrea discussed the day's challenges with Arthur. Her job didn't sound like fun to Erik. By now he knew he was supposed to help her - White Wolf had been clear about this. Erik learned to recognize when Andrea's energy was low or when she looked overly tired or stressed. He often found a way to give her a break, and get her mind off her work.

Erik knew instinctively when she needed him. If Andrea needed to relax, he would say to himself, "I'll just give her a hug with my nose." Whenever he did this, Erik could feel Andrea's stiff body begin to loosen up. She would always return his hug by stroking his coat and burying her head in his fluffy neck. The long, deep breaths she took as she burrowed her face in his fur let him know he was helping her. Andrea knew this too.

Erik was settling into his job quite well. Sometimes, if he thought Andrea needed to play, he would bring her one of his toys and shake it to get her attention. If he was successful, that meant a good run around the house playing "go get the ball" as she would toss it from room to room. If they could get the Princess to join in the play, they all would have a rambunctious run through the house, knocking over chairs and occasionally breaking something. It was okay though; as long as Andrea was involved in the fun, the dogs knew they wouldn't get in trouble. Andrea grew to appreciate the diversion.

One Saturday at home, Andrea was on a phone call with her boss. To Erik, she looked and sounded very worried. She was talking about an unhappy client and was lost in the conversation. Erik tried to get her to throw the ball for him by dropping the wet, sloppy thing into her lap. Andrea ignored him – repeatedly. Erik was puzzled. He thought, "I'm usually pretty good at this, and she's not paying any attention to me. She really needs to play."

The Princess saw it coming. "Don't do it, Erik. That's not the way to get her to play with you!"

"Well, she's not responding to any of my usual tricks. I've got to do my job and get her to be less tense. If getting in trouble gets her mind off her work, then I've got to do it," Erik replied.

Erik's old wolf-dog ways emerged as he remembered an approach that had worked successfully for him long ago. He walked across the room and waited until Andrea looked up from her call. Then, he lifted his leg and peed on the side of the sofa!

Erik was fully aware of what he had done, and his tactic worked – at least he thought so at first. Andrea quickly hung up the phone and shouted at Erik, "Bad dog! What a bad, bad boy!"

Andrea got the cleaning supplies out and furiously scrubbed to clean the yellow stain from the sofa. Then, she stopped and thought about what had happened. She realized what Erik was doing. "You sure have a funny – and very frustrating – way of getting my attention."

"Good," thought Erik. "She's finally starting to understand my job."

Erik was working very hard, but he still made mistakes. Both Erik and Andrea were learning.

Arthur entered the house just as Andrea was putting the cleaning supplies away. He noticed her posture immediately and thought she must be frustrated about something. The Princess looked especially smug.

"What happened here?" Arthur asked.

Andrea relayed the story. When she finished, Arthur wanted to tell her that Erik was trying to get through to her the same way that he often tried. He wanted to hold her and tell her that life was too precious to waste feeling stress over someone's unreasonable demands on her time and energy. He wanted to tell her, right then and there, what was important in life.

But he knew better, and he was grateful that Erik could get away with what he could not. Arthur was older than Andrea and while they were partners and peers in most every way, he had gained wisdom that he could not impart to another. Andrea had to learn this for herself.

•

Erik hoped that White Wolf would come to him on the night of the sofa incident. He had begun to think of this presence as his teacher because each brief communication gave him new knowledge. Tonight, he had many questions. He got his wish and White Wolf appeared.

"White Wolf, does Andrea get messages like I do from you?"

"Oh yes, Erik. I send her many messages in many forms. Sometimes they take the shape of clouds in the sky or animals that cross her path as she walks with you through the neighborhood. I even send her messages through songs she hears. But often she can't sense them, or make sense of them enough to express the feelings they convey."

"Why?"

"She forgot how."

"That seems silly," Erik thought. Then he said, "It's easy for me. It's just like my other instincts. Powerful and certain."

White Wolf replied, "Andrea forgot how to sense her intuition and express her true feelings when she was a little girl growing up. Many children do. It's our job – your job – to help her remember how to listen."

"That sounds like important work," Erik said.

"It is," White Wolf responded. "It's the most

important work you will ever do. That's enough for you to take in now, Erik. I'll be back again and we will continue this."

"White Wolf, can I please ask you just one more question?"

"Go ahead Erik."

"Sometimes I know Andrea needs something and I can't figure out what to do to help her. What should I do at those times?"

"Just love her with all your heart." And White Wolf disappeared.

REFLECTIONS
Hearing the Whispers

You could say life was on auto pilot for Andrea. She had what many young women consider success – a loving relationship with Arthur and a challenging job with potential to grow and build a career. She was generally happy.

Like many people her age, she didn't know what she didn't know. While life "worked" most of the time, she had a nagging sense of something greater than what was before her. There had been synchronicities, events that gave her pause and whispered of more to come. At the same time, she had neither a compass nor a crystal ball.

Arthur and Erik's love carried her. Finding Arthur was no more a result of luck than finding Erik had been. So far in her young life, she had made at least two very important choices, choices that resulted from paying attention to what was in her heart.

The connection to Andrea's innate knowing was not entirely severed. She was waking up from her state of emotional dullness. While it would be a long time before she had a conscious ability to integrate mind, body and spirit – fully align head and heart – she was at least beginning to have inklings of her purpose in life. Always driven to succeed, Andrea was not content to stay on a path of incremental growth in a "career" that did not really spark passion in her.

You've probably heard the saying: "When the student is ready the teacher appears." One such teacher, Linda, appeared in Andrea's life. What looked like an ordinary action became a turning point. She signed up for a workshop offered by Linda's company.

It was a typical course offered to managers; techniques for productivity improvement and time management, coupled with personal goal setting. For Andrea, this was no ordinary experience. While up to this point Andrea was quite goal-focused in terms of business objectives and accomplishments, this was the first time she'd considered life goals in this manner. The personal focus as well as a caring and determined facilitator (who later became a mentor and friend) allowed her to explore her intrinsic motivators, skills and talents. It helped Andrea examine life so far, and catalog achievements, disappointments and desires.

One of the realizations Andrea awoke to was her innate talent for helping others learn and grow. She realized that for her, much of life's most satisfying work as well as play involved teaching.

When she was a young girl, Andrea did not play "house" with her dolls as many of her friends did. Instead she played "school." Each afternoon, after returning home from a long day at St. Mary's grade school, Andrea lined up her dolls on the edge of her bed, dragged a large blackboard from her closet, and opened the teacher's manuals donated by a great aunt who was a former elementary school teacher. Andrea conducted class until dinner time, often sharing the accomplishments and escapades of the dolls with her parents over the evening meal.

Andrea's role as a teacher expanded and her entrepreneurial spirit emerged alongside it. In college, she ran a fledgling business tutoring fellow students and progressed to teach formal classes during graduate school. As she looked back at her short career, the times she was most engaged and most fulfilled were the times she was helping other people learn and grow. Armed with this realization, during this life-changing workshop, Andrea set one of the most important goals in her life – to start a business of her own in which she helped people align their unique gifts and talents with the work and life they were passionate about.

Reflect on the dimensions of your life. What makes your heart sing? Are there activities you do during which time stands still? Is there one thing you do that brings joy, regardless of the content or context? Is there a pastime, a job or hobby that is timeless, one that you have enjoyed consistently at many times in your life? What does that activity do for you?

Are there things you do that feel dull or like drudgery? Are there things you are "good at" yet do not enjoy?

What patterns have you identified?

CHAPTER NINE

As time passed and they got to know each other better, Erik and the Princess became good friends. The Princess was the more mature of the two dogs and was now a gracious old lady. Erik could sense her body aging rapidly. They talked more these days about important things, like their experiences together and their family. They remembered all the fun they had shared in the places they had lived and even laughed about Erik's mischief.

"Do you remember the trip we took to the beach where you taught me to run toward the waves, but to race back before I got wet?" Erik asked the Princess.

"Yes, and you got to be pretty good at it, too. You could always outrun me back to the dry sand. I won't forget the time you double-dared me and I stayed out too long. I got drenched by that wave! My fur smelled really bad until Andrea got home and gave me a bath."

The family had taken many vacations, sometimes to the ocean and sometimes to the mountains. There had been long walks in the woods with autumn leaves crunching beneath their feet, and, if the dogs were lucky, they found an occasional squirrel to chase up a tree.

Erik had taught the Princess how to have fun like a dog and she had taught him how to be a gentleman – or at least she had tried. Erik loved the Princess for her regal unselfishness. They had had good times together.

These days, there wasn't as much romping and chasing as there used to be. Erik understood the Princess was having more difficulty getting up and moving about. He sometimes lay with her for hours in front of the sunny window, just napping and gazing at the view. The Princess shared things with him she had never talked about before, as if she were trying to teach him everything she knew before her death.

She told Erik, "Dogs are sent to humans to aid them. Sometimes it's because they need a friend, sometimes it's to teach the human through their shared experiences; and, sometimes they come just for companionship. Humans, like dogs, need to feel loved and dogs are the very best creatures on earth at providing unconditional love."

With the Princess' help, Erik better understood the role he had been sent to play in Andrea's life. Sometimes it seemed to him that the Princess was almost as smart as White Wolf.

Erik appreciated his job now even more. He deeply respected his friend, the Princess, and was grateful to her for being his patient teacher. Sometimes he felt bad about all the mischief he had gotten into.

One day Erik said, "Princess, when I was younger, you used to scold me for doing bad things like peeing in inappropriate places and chewing Andrea and Arthur's belongings. I always thought you were a 'goody four paws' that didn't know how to have fun. Now I admire your manners and obedience. I wish I could be more like you."

"Erik, you must never wish you were someone else," the Princess stated emphatically. "You are perfect the way you are. And in case you think that I never did anything bad, let me tell you some stories."

Erik settled back and listened as the Princess told him how trampling her former owner's petunias had almost cost her her life many years ago. "If Lucy had not shared my story with Andrea that day, I don't think I would be alive right now."

"Wow," Erik said. "When I joined our family, I thought you had lived in luxury all your life. You're a rescued dog just like me!"

"Tell me another story Princess!" Erik said excitedly.

"Well, remember how you used to try to run away? I did that just once. And I thought I would never find Andrea and Arthur again."

"Oh, that sounds scary! Tell me what happened."

"Andrea and Arthur took me on a long weekend trip to San Diego. We had a great time. We stayed in a fancy hotel suite and went for long walks on the beach. On the last day, they wanted to go shopping in Old Town San Diego. Apparently they didn't allow dogs in that shopping area."

"Arthur said, 'Princess, we are going to park the car under this shade tree and leave you here for about an hour. We'll open the windows a bit so you will have plenty of fresh air.' They pressed the buttons to lower the windows a few inches and then turned off the car's engine. They locked the doors and waved goodbye. I settled in for one of my afternoon naps in the driver's seat. I liked that place best because I could smell Arthur all around me."

"Just as soon as I got comfortable, I heard a noise.

It was a meow! There was a cat just outside the car. Well, I usually can control myself, but something just came over me. I stood up against the front door and scratched the window. To my amazement, it came down. Fell right into the slot where it disappears when they press the buttons!"

"I leaned out the window to catch a glimpse of the cat and before I knew it, I slid all the way to the ground. The cat, a really mean-looking yellow cat with black feet, took off. I chased after her."

"I chased her for a long time, up and down streets, until she ducked underneath a large truck parked in a driveway. All at once I came to my senses and realized I didn't know where I was or how to get back to the car. I quickly forgot about the cat and concentrated on finding Arthur and Andrea. I thought they had to be close, so I just sniffed the air to get their scent. But I was very afraid. I didn't know if I would be able to find them."

"It's a good thing we have such powerful noses," Erik added.

"Yes, it is a good thing. Suddenly, I smelled them, and thought they must be walking down the next street over. I ran through traffic to get there. When they saw me trotting down the street, they started screaming at me – they were frantic. I thought they were going to be very angry but they just acted happy to see me. I knew how much they loved me then, and I decided that I must make sure we stayed together – always."

"What happened next?" asked Erik.

"Not too much. We went back to the car and left for home in Arizona shortly after that. It was a fun trip, because the window was broken and the wind blew in my face the whole way home – about six hours."

"Lucky dog!" Erik said. "Princess?"

"What Erik?" Princess replied, sounding a bit exhausted.

"Why didn't you tell me these stories before? Why didn't you try to teach me these lessons sooner?"

"It wouldn't have made a difference, Erik. When we're young, we think we know everything. We don't of course, but some lessons just have to be learned first-hand. Each of us has our own path to follow, and we learn as we encounter obstacles that appear to get in our way. The obstacles are really tools through which we learn."

Erik wanted to ask the Princess more about that – maybe it would help him with Andrea. But when he glanced at her, he hesitated. She looked very tired from all this story-telling. Erik let her rest and soon both were fast asleep.

CHAPTER TEN

Eventually, Erik came to realize that the Princess was very ill and her body frail. Her once-vibrant life energy was fading. She was preparing to die. He loved her and stayed close by in case she needed him.

"Please promise me you will be here for Arthur when I am gone, Erik. He will miss me terribly. I don't want him to hurt – I love him so." The Princess made Erik promise. His heart was hurting, too, as he thought of losing her friendship. It didn't matter. He had to be strong – he had made the promise.

Arthur was also aware that his beloved Princess was preparing to leave. He knew she loved him with all her might and was hanging on to life just to spare him the pain of being without her.

Arthur had to muster the courage to talk to her.

One day, the Princess could no longer walk. Arthur gathered her in his arms and placed her in her favorite spot by the window where she could see the birds and trees outside. He held her close and told her, "I understand why you're holding on, my sweet Princess. But it's not fair for you to stay here for me when it's your time to leave the earth. I love you. When you're ready, I'll let you go. I know I will see you again."

With those words she sent him love, and closed her eyes.

CHAPTER ELEVEN

Andrea was sitting in the hotel atrium when her cell phone rang. Arthur's number appeared on the display but the trembling voice didn't sound like him. "The Princess is gone, Andrea. She died tonight . . . " The rest of his words drowned in sobs.

Andrea had been on edge all week, trying to concentrate on the business plan review she was conducting in Baton Rouge while keeping in close touch with Arthur. When she'd left home, the Princess was failing fast and Arthur had seemed to be the one in denial. She had tried to talk to him, to get him to let the Princess go. But he was in so much pain, and there was nothing Andrea could do to make it go away.

Several months before, Andrea and Arthur had noticed that the Princess was limping. They immediately visited the veterinarian, who determined that she had a fungal infection common to the Arizona desert. In the late 1980's, a diagnosis of Valley Fever was grim. The treatments were often more destructive than the disease and there were limited options.

When the veterinarian first examined the Princess, he offered three potential causes: arthritis, bone cancer or Valley Fever. He leaned toward the latter two until further tests could confirm a diagnosis.

The thought that the Princess could have cancer was too much for Andrea to consider and she put it out of her mind. When the doctor called to say that the Valley Fever test was positive, she responded with a loud sigh. "Oh thank God." The doctor quickly replied with concern in his voice. "Well, Andrea, this is not exactly good news. Valley Fever is a very serious illness."

Upon hearing those chilling words, Andrea kicked into action. She busied herself researching various treatments and the prognosis for the disease with a clinical, unemotional approach.

While the family tried many options, Arthur could only watch as his once-healthy dog declined rapidly. There were times he thought Andrea didn't seem to notice. She could even appear cold as she played with Erik and regarded both dogs as if nothing was wrong. Other times she seemed upset and distracted, tears seeping out like a leaky faucet at odd moments without explanation.

REFLECTIONS
Fear

It would be inaccurate to say that Andrea was uncaring or unfeeling at this time. In fact, the opposite was true. Her two sources of pain, the illness and potential death of the sweet and loving Princess, as well as Arthur's deep sadness, overwhelmed her. She didn't know how to express or even become present to the feelings she was experiencing. When people deny emotions, they don't go away. The death of the Princess added to the stockpile of unexplored fears.

Fear was a state Andrea would not fully understand until Erik's death years later. She could not have named what she was afraid of at the time of the Princess' death because she was in denial. Eckhart Tolle says that failure to accept the moment at hand is the very thing that creates suffering. Peace comes as a result of acceptance, not avoidance.

Each of us is connected to the world around us. A ripple in one person's consciousness disrupts the web of life force in subtle, yet, profound ways. Love breeds more love, fear begets fear. There are countless examples of this principle at play in disciplines like economics and politics as well as in families, communities and societies. Unexpressed emotion does not stay dormant. What we don't express productively, we act out in ways that are damaging to ourselves and the world around us.

Some talk out their feelings, others cry, dance, or engage in rituals that allow for expression. When these things work, it's because we move from a conceptual experience in our minds to full engagement with what exists in the moment. Transformation requires integration of body, mind and spirit.

Consider a source of pain, anxiety or fear in your life right now. In no more than a paragraph or two, describe it.

Re-read the passage you wrote and then answer these questions.

What part of it is true in this very moment?

Are there any parts of it that are stories you have "made up" about something that happened?

Are there any parts of it that possibly or likely will happen but have not happened yet?

Breathe in deeply. As you exhale slowly, become aware of your body, head to toe. With your feet planted firmly on the ground, take in another deep breath. This time, as you exhale, become aware of the reality of this situation you chose to focus on.

How are you experiencing it at this moment?

Name the emotion you feel. Where in your body is the feeling most pronounced?

This place you are in is pure consciousness. It is the only place from which to choose what's next.

CHAPTER TWELVE

"I miss the Princess," thought Erik. "She taught me many lessons. And now I need to take care of Andrea and Arthur by myself." Erik was deep in his thoughts. "I love them both, and I know that Arthur especially needs me."

Andrea kept asking, "Are you ready for a new puppy, Arthur?" But Arthur wasn't ready. He even got tears in his eyes when she mentioned it.

Erik thought, "I have enough love for both of them." And so, he began the loving task of caring for Andrea and Arthur.

Andrea's job was based in Minnesota and she traveled home to her family in South Carolina each weekend. The family was living near the ocean in Charleston. It was Erik's favorite home ever, and soon became a time filled with much fun and joy. Andrea was away a lot and when she was gone, Arthur and Erik were pals. He would come home from work at the end of the day, grab the leash and Erik, and head for the beach.

You would think that Erik would be terrified at the thought of getting wet given how much he feared baths, but when the giant waves splashed to shore, Erik remembered what the Princess had taught him about the waves and always had a plan. He would tempt fate and run to the edge of the waves, playing a game with them, and then run back as fast as he could – which was always just in time! She had taught him well.

He also made games with the funny, fast-walking birds on the beach, chasing them as they rushed in to grab the prizes left in the sand by the retreating waves. He loved chasing crabs as they scampered back to the safety of the water. What fun he and Arthur had!

Ocean walks were good for Andrea, too, and she took Erik to the beach as often as possible. Erik felt like a very lucky dog.

When Andrea walked on the beach with Erik, she could lose herself in the sounds and steadiness of the waves' patterns. She listened as the water crashed to the shore, then retreated back to the sea with whooshes and trickles. She felt the wind in her hair and the fine ocean spray on her body. The sun warmed her face.

For Andrea, time stood still on the beach. On those walks, Erik thought Andrea seemed quite different than she had in the early days, when her mind was often distracted and her heart unavailable to anyone but him and Arthur. "This is because of me!" he said to himself, very satisfied with his work so far.

Andrea noticed the change in Erik more than she noticed the change in herself. As he'd matured beyond the antics of his youth, he had become like a wise friend to her. His calming presence was palpable and she marveled at how safe and content she felt in his presence. While she might not yet have used the word "teacher," Andrea knew this dog had a purpose in her life.

Erik imagined that White Wolf, too, was pleased with his work. But he still had a lot of questions. One night, exhausted from a long beach romp, Erik called upon his teacher. He always came when Erik made the request. With each visit, White Wolf seemed more and more real.

"White Wolf, a long time ago you told me Andrea had forgotten how to sense love like yours and had forgotten how to listen to the wisdom that is part of All That Is."

"Yes Erik, that's right. When Andrea was a little girl, she had what her family called 'imaginary friends.' There were five of them; they all had names and personalities. She talked to them and imagined that they were part of her life. She had conversations with them like the ones you have with me. She shared all her feelings and ideas with them, and they helped her learn about herself and other people. When Andrea was very young, she was most sensitive and creative."

"What happened?" Erik asked.

"The same thing that happens to many children," White Wolf replied. "Well-meaning adults train them to be logical and less sensitive. Parents teach them to follow rules and keep their feelings to themselves. The parents are usually just trying to help. But some children learn that their own feelings aren't useful at all. They learn that thinking and doing is more valuable than experiencing. Most kids experience very painful things growing up and they learn ways of dealing with this. Some block pain and bad feelings; others learn to suffer through quietly. Still others learn to express it in productive ways, though that doesn't always happen until they are much older, like Andrea is now."

"White Wolf, you said Andrea had imaginary friends growing up. Did she have real friends too?"

"Oh yes. She even had a best friend, her cousin Julie. They were about the same age. They were almost inseparable, even though they lived in different towns. They told each other all of their dreams and ideas. Slowly, as Andrea grew older, Julie's presence in her life replaced the imaginary friends."

"One night, a tragedy occurred. Andrea's mother got a phone call from Julie's dad. He told her that Julie had died in a car accident."

"Oh White Wolf, Andrea lost her best friend!" Erik said.

"Yes. Andrea was fifteen when that happened. She had been sitting with her parents watching television when her whole world changed in just an instant. As you would expect, she was shocked by the news. I remember that time well; I watched her suffer and I could not reach her. She sat in a chair and began to shake when her mother told her what had happened. It was a turning point in her young life . . . and not for the better."

Erik interrupted White Wolf's recollection. "I bet Andrea was feeling very sad."

"That was the problem, Erik. She buried her feelings instead of expressing them. She learned how to hold back tears and push the feelings aside. They were very painful and it frightened her. It was as if Andrea flipped a switch and learned to live in her head instead of her heart. Sometimes her heart would open up when she listened to her favorite music, especially after Julie's death. She didn't go to Julie's funeral. She stayed home alone and listened to the same song playing over and over again. That's why I send her music to help her remember."

"Oh, White Wolf, Andrea loves music," Erik noted. "Sometimes she plays it so loud it hurts my ears!"

White Wolf smiled, then continued . . . "Some years after Julie's death, Andrea's dad became very ill. He died just after she graduated from college; Andrea was still young. By that time, though, she had become very skilled at hiding her feelings and she didn't know any other way. Looking in from the outside, most people thought she was strong and resilient. Some even thought she was uncaring. What was really happening is that those feelings of grief she'd buried were adding to the sadness and pain of losing her dad. It was all too much at once and she shut down yet again."

"Why is this important, White Wolf?"

"Because, Erik, when people block or bury painful

feelings, they also block out joy, love and inspiration – all the things humans experience when they are at their best. Being able to experience the moment at hand – whatever that moment brings – is a key to becoming a fully creative and compassionate human being. Andrea will need that capacity for the work she will do in future years, helping others find purpose in life's challenges. Your love for her, and hers for you, will be the force that allows her to regain that ability. You will teach her how."

"I'm not sure I understand."

"You will, Erik. You will."

REFLECTIONS
Frozen In Time

Every individual deals with the aftermath of learning about the death of a loved one in a unique way. Some naturally work through the phases of grief in linear or non-linear patterns, experiencing emotions like anger, sadness, and depression along the way. Getting stuck in any of these phases, or avoiding the emotion entirely, creates emotional and often physical blocks. Frozen emotions get stuck in our bodies, creating all manner of side effects. The phrase "getting to the other side of grief" is symbolic of the channel that must open for the journey to the place of acceptance.

When Andrea learned of Julie's death she made an unconscious choice to block the pain. She froze it in time and carried it into her future.

CHAPTER THIRTEEN

Andrea's Minnesota job was filled with contradictions. In one sense it was a huge achievement, a promotion usually reserved for someone with much more experience, and Andrea rose to the challenge from the first day. On the other hand, it tested her mettle in every way.

Andrea and a small group of executives were running a spin-off hotel company fraught with challenges in a difficult economy. The odds were against them but they were nearing the point of breakthrough just as Andrea's resolve to start her own business strengthened.

Andrea had taken this position with a clear goal to leave in two years, prepared to start a business in which she could impact people's lives more directly than she could in the hotel business. She even referred to this last promotion as evidence of living a "charmed life," having been offered the opportunity to learn and grow rapidly in ways that she eventually could put into practice in her own company.

As the time approached, fear and apprehension came and went. Andrea had no doubt she would be successful – her only worry was how long would it take. While she was fortunate that Arthur's income would carry them through the start-up phase of the business, she felt the heavy responsibility that the significant financial stress would introduce to their lives. And as they often do, well-meaning friends did as much to dissuade her as they did to encourage her, telling her how hard it would be.

In the fall of 1992, Andrea took the plunge. She resigned her position and agreed to consult with her former company while preparing her own business plans. The decision to begin had been made; now the question was where to launch the business.

•

One beautiful November morning, Erik decided it was time for Andrea to take a much-needed day off. She was sitting stiffly at her desk, and it looked to him like she was worrying again. She was. At this time in her life, Andrea was beginning to recognize and harness the synchronistic opportunities that fell into place before her. Still, she agonized over decisions, analyzing and second-guessing them to the point of exhaustion before giving in to the innate wisdom that had been there all along. On this particular day, Andrea was doing just that. As she considered the decisions ahead, recent memories gnawed at her. She was lost in thought, recalling a series of experiences while traveling.

The commute had been challenging and the extended time away had created tensions. Early on, Andrea made a decision that time with Arthur and Erik on the weekends was too precious for her to arrive harried and exhausted from traveling. She made a conscious effort to relax and make business travel an adventure, and she was successful with this much of the time.

When Andrea flew home to South Carolina from Minnesota each weekend, she usually made a connection through Atlanta. Though she had never set foot outside the airport, she was awed by the view of the city at night from the airplane window seat. Oddly, each time the pilot announced, "We've been cleared to land in Atlanta," Andrea felt a strong shiver and her eyes welled up with tears. It became more pronounced with time, so much so that she became concerned that other passengers might see this odd display of emotion.

Curious, she was anxious to visit this city on the ground. An opportunity presented itself in October.

Andrea needed to drive her car and belongings from Minneapolis to Charleston after resigning from her job, and she stopped in St. Louis to get her mother, making the trip a vacation for both of them. After leaving St. Louis, they planned an overnight stay in Atlanta. Andrea chose a location in the heart of the city, the Omni Hotel in CNN Center. They arrived late at night and immediately went to bed.

The next morning, the choice to visit Atlanta seemed to reinforce the airplane experiences. After breakfast, Andrea decided she would like to take a CNN Studio Tour before leaving the city. As she entered the long tour line in CNN Center's atrium, she had the same sensation she had felt so many times landing in Atlanta, but this instance was heightened by the music coming from a live band playing on a stage near the center. The small group was delivering a remarkably good cover version of Elton John's then-popular hit, "The One."

Lately, Andrea had been noticing that music was

having a powerful effect on her, much the way it did as she was growing up. Now, standing in line in the immense space, the music seemed to echo loudly in her heart. The intense feeling was accompanied by a vision. Andrea imagined herself working right there in CNN Center. It was strong and felt so right . . . but how?

Andrea was becoming convinced that she needed to launch her business in Atlanta. Doing so would mean that Arthur would need to be transferred or find a new job in the new city. This would be no small task, as he really did enjoy work in Charleston. Andrea wrestled with the strong message she was receiving to move to Atlanta versus the feeling of unfairness to Arthur.

CHAPTER FOURTEEN

Erik ran to the open closet and pulled his leash off the shelf.

After Erik made several attempts at dragging his leash around the room and tossing it at her feet, Andrea finally picked up on his request and jolted back to reality. Erik was delighted when she said, "Big Dog, let's go to the beach!" He liked it when Andrea called him Big Dog.

She knew that she would not be able to make a good decision by worrying over her desk; she needed fresh ocean air and a day of play with her best friend. She read the excitement on Erik's face. "I know, sweet friend – we both need a break. We'll walk as long as we wish, all day if we want. Thank you, Erik. Your timing is perfect. You seem to know just what I need."

Erik was dancing. "A magical day," he thought. "No deadlines! No hurrying about!" It turned out the day *was* magical.

As they walked, Andrea, her head filled with concerns still drifting about, noted that Erik was no longer beside her on the beach. He had run ahead and was dancing and barking to get her attention. When she focused her eyes on the subject of his excitement, she saw sand dollars. Not just one or two, but hundreds of white sand dollars scattered across the sand.

Andrea hurried to catch up with him. As she neared the collection of sand dollars, she marveled at the bounty before her. She slowed her walk and began picking up as many sand dollars as her pockets would accommodate. After gathering all her pockets would hold, she paused and ran her hand over one perfectly formed specimen. She looked down and locked her gaze on Erik. Their eyes met.

"That's it!" Andrea exclaimed, and bent to give her dog a hug. She felt that now-familiar shiver again. "Erik, you helped me find the answer!" Jubilantly, Erik and Andrea raced and danced up and down the beach.

Andrea had set out that day to clear her mind of worry about her decision. The sand dollars had provided the needed distraction. And then – as if a light bulb had been turned on in her head – she knew. The sand dollars themselves were a sign to her that the move to Atlanta was the right one. How they would get there was but a minor detail.

Legend has it that the five tiny, white bird-shaped bones inside the sand dollar represent five white doves, each waiting to spread goodwill and peace – at home, at work, at play and with each other. It became apparent to Andrea. The doves that fell from the broken sand dollars represented the work she would do to help people learn and grow.

As Erik watched Andrea he thought, "Just as she and I found each other, Andrea is now finding the pathway to her life's passion – helping others in their growth. I know I've been an instrument in that discovery, and I feel good about my work."

Erik continued to think, "And, I know I'm achieving my mission – my journey – and that feels good too." He straightened his head, gazed steadily at the horizon and received confirmation from White Wolf. Erik's own intuition was accurate, and Andrea's was finally coming back to life.

Reluctantly, Andrea realized it was time to bring this outing to a close. But this special day did not end at the beach.

Andrea led Erik to their car and they piled in.

Sandy and sweaty, it occurred to her that they were making a mess in Arthur's prized 280Z. She smiled at the thought of him complaining about it later, while secretly enjoying the fact that she shared his love for his quirky old car. She was glad she'd chosen this vehicle today. What it lacked in modern conveniences like adequate air conditioning, it more than made up for in soul. Soon, they were speeding away from the beach, T-tops down, wind in their hair.

The sun was setting over the marsh as they drove. Andrea turned up the stereo's volume as she caught the opening notes from "The One." *There it was again!* In that moment, the lyrics seemed to be written precisely about the bond she had with her dog.

Erik, sitting in the back seat, noticed Andrea looking at him through the rear view mirror. The expression on her face changed suddenly as the music played on.

"Am I getting some kind of message I should be paying attention to?" she silently asked herself.

All at once, Andrea recognized that Erik had brought her this far. Erik sensed her acknowledgment even before the tears began. That day, as the song goes, the pieces finally fit for Andrea.

Erik's unconditional love for Andrea was palpable. For those few moments in the car, time stood still.

Every sense was triggered. Blazing sunlight burned the smell of low-country tidewater. The music and lyrics took a heady experience to a transformational level.

"Maybe she's finally beginning to understand my purpose in her life," Erik thought.

Andrea *was* beginning to understand Erik's unselfish mission. He had suffered much as a young dog. Andrea knew that none of that mattered to him, not as long as he was with her.

Andrea smiled, thinking about the sand dollars piled up in the passenger seat next to her. They served as a symbol that the new business plans were solid. Somehow, the events of this day confirmed that her instincts about the location were right too. Erik had given her a beautiful gift. If not for him, she would never have felt the freedom to spend the day wandering the beach – and she would not have discovered the message of the sand dollars.

•

Andrea was anxious to show Arthur the sand dollars and to discuss a move to Atlanta. As she entered the foyer of their condo, Arthur met her with excitement in his eyes.

"Andrea, guess what?" he asked eagerly.

"What?" Andrea smiled at the thought that his mood matched hers, but she never could have predicted what he would say next.

"Well," Arthur began. "I just got a call from my friend Greg in Atlanta. He was transferred there last summer and wants me to interview for a job." Arthur held his breath as he watched Andrea's response.

She grinned from ear to ear and hugged Arthur until her arms ached. He took that as a good sign. "I'll tell Greg I can fly over this weekend."

Andrea had indeed been cleared to land in Atlanta.

Late that night, Erik and White Wolf talked about the moment in the car when Andrea had experienced his unconditional love.

"White Wolf, I think I understand what you were trying to teach me about the present moment being the time of great creativity."

"Yes. And you know something, Erik? Dogs live in the present moment all the time. They don't fret and worry like the humans do. That's one of the reasons you were chosen as Andrea's teacher."

"Ah, yes." Erik thought, pleased. White Wolf was pleased too.

REFLECTIONS
Being Present

We've all heard the adages:

"Everything you need to know is available to you."
"God will handle the details."
"Never bet against the person with pure intention."

What is the mechanism at play here, and why do these so-called universal principles seem to only work some of the time?

At any given moment, we each have a choice to step into an experience from the heart and feel it with all our senses, or to remain inside our heads, thinking about it – or think about the past or future events related to it. This condition of living experientially (in the now) versus conceptually (in our heads) applies to mundane experiences such as airplane flights or to seemingly more important events such as a decision about one's future career.

While the human brain is a remarkable thing, access to our innate knowing, our intuition and the source of creativity does not reside there. When Andrea relaxed and became present to the sights and sounds from her airplane seat, she received a message through her senses – senses that were waking up after a long period of numbness in which her clever brain had convinced her it was all she needed.

Fortunately, she paid attention to the messages, and with Erik's help, she used the same process of becoming present at the beach to clarify her intention to move to Atlanta. It seems almost counter-intuitive, because that's the point at which many of us would try to "figure things out" – the very thing Andrea was doing at her desk when Erik interrupted.

The transformation at the beach was simple but profound. Atlanta moved from "thought" or "idea" to commitment. This intentionality was the seedbed in which the "details" manifested. This famous passage reminds us of the principle.

> "The moment one definitely commits oneself, then providence moves too. All sorts of things occur to help one that would never otherwise have occurred. A whole stream of events issues from the decision, raising in one's

favor all manner of unforeseen incidents and meetings and material assistance which no man could have dreamed would have come his way."

W. H. Murray in The Scottish Himalayan Expedition, 1951, referring to German poet Goethe's couplet:

"Whatever you can do or dream you can, begin it. Boldness has genius, power and magic in it!"

While there are many wonderful tools and techniques for becoming more present – things like meditation, yoga – or hugging your dog – it does not have to be an "event." Being present is the human condition. Try it now.

Become aware of your body and your breath. Can you feel your arms? Your feet? What do you see? What do you hear? Notice any smells, tastes or other sensations. What are you feeling right now? Where in your body is this feeling most pronounced?

It's really that simple.

CHAPTER FIFTEEN

The symbolic sand dollar experience, combined with the seemingly coincidental job interview Arthur was offered, sealed Andrea's certainty about the decision to move to Atlanta. In fact, she was so confident that she began packing the family's belongings as soon as Arthur left on his short trip. He returned to the clutter of boxes and a half-empty kitchen.

Arthur opened his mouth to speak and then hesitated. He smiled when he recognized the lyrics coming from the too-loud stereo. Ray Charles had been as enamored with Georgia as Andrea was. Arthur regained his stance and asked, incredulously:

"What on earth are you doing Andrea? I had an interview, nothing more. I hope I get the job, of course – but I won't know for several days!"

"You'll get the job," Andrea replied. "And we have a lot of work to do to prepare for the move, so I thought I would get started." With a warm smile she added, "Now can you help me wrap these glasses? I want to get the table cleared for dinner."

Dumbfounded, Arthur began wrapping glassware, preparing for a move in which nothing was certain except the resolve of his wife. As it turned out, that resolve proved accurate.

•

Following the move to Atlanta, Erik watched as everything seemed to fall into place for Andrea and Arthur. Andrea was very busy in her new business, and it was work that fulfilled her. Her first client was Turner Broadcasting, located in CNN Center, the same building where months before her premonition about the move to Atlanta had been so strong.

"I'm so glad they're happy," Erik thought. Arthur enjoyed his new job and Erik was content that his work with Andrea was on track.

The only problem was that their first home in Atlanta was a small condo in the city. It was not the best place for a dog – and to make matters worse, Arthur had finally agreed to get a puppy. Andrea presented him with a four-month-old Samoyed named Sasha just as they were settling into the new condo.

"A new puppy under foot, and I need to run!" Erik kept thinking. "This place is too small for me. And that puppy is driving me crazy!"

And then a mischievous thought crossed Erik's mind, but immediately he was stopped. It was as if the Princess had come back to remind him. "Okay, okay . . . I get it." He spoke as if the Princess were there. "I've got to have patience with Sasha just like you did with me."

Andrea realized that Erik and Sasha were cooped up too much when she came home one day and found every upstairs wooden window sill destroyed. This time though, the culprit was the puppy Sasha! Fortunately for Erik, his pleading eyes sent a message to Andrea. She understood and upon investigation confirmed that Sasha had chewed the wood.

Erik overheard Andrea and Arthur talking about the costly repairs that were needed. He felt bad; maybe he could have stopped Sasha, but he needed a yard, too – a big yard. If Sasha's bad behavior could help him get a yard, Erik would encourage her to keep chewing on things!

Andrea knew he needed to run and she knew the

young puppy needed exercise too. She promised Erik, "I'm going to get you a yard!"

Andrea, Arthur, Erik and Sasha began looking for a new home – a bigger home with a fenced backyard. The exploring meant lots of car rides, which Erik loved. Sasha had learned to open the back windows by pushing the button on the door.

"Finally," Erik thought, "something good is coming from that puppy."

As he held his head out the top of the car window, the wind blew in Erik's face so hard he could barely breathe – but what fun! His ears blew back. He let his tongue dangle because that's what dogs are supposed to do when they hang their heads out the window. His eyes watered. Arthur fussed about the slobbery window, but Andrea told him to relax. She knew what Erik loved.

One day, they visited a house in Lawrenceville, a suburb of Atlanta. As soon as everyone got out of the car, Erik knew this was the perfect home for them. He strained on his leash, pulling Andrea around to the back of the house. There, the most magnificent fenced-in backyard was waiting. The yard had trees, lots of them! It had a little hill and all around was plenty of grass. There were areas of shade and areas of sun. Erik thought to himself, "It doesn't get any better than this!"

Andrea and Arthur must have sensed his excitement as they laughed at the joyful expression on his face. Andrea told him, "Okay boy. This is it. This is going to be your new home and all this space is yours."

Arthur added that Erik needed to share his new yard with Sasha. Erik and Andrea just looked at each other and smiled.

Then Andrea said to Arthur, "I guess we better go take a look at the inside of the house since we've decided to buy it." And so they did.

•

The new home in Lawrenceville was absolutely perfect. Arthur installed two doggy doors this time. One was a passage from the kitchen to the basement and the other from the basement to the yard. Erik and Sasha could go in and out as much as they liked. Everything seemed just right, yet there was a problem lurking. The carpet in the new house was white and the dirt outside was red clay typical of that part of Georgia.

Now, being that Sasha didn't know about the red clay and she had lots of puppy energy, and being that Erik was not a scientist, the two had no idea how much trouble they could get into by mixing white carpet with red clay. Erik had matured over the years, but sometimes the puppy Sasha brought out the worst in him.

One particular day it had rained all morning, and by afternoon Erik and Sasha were ready to be outside. The heavy rain had mixed with the red clay, creating glue-like mud that stuck to the bottoms of their paws. It looked like rusty red finger paint. Erik and Sasha raced through the wet grass, which felt cool to their feet. They found a chipmunk's burrowed hole and furiously dug into it as if they were bloodhounds, slinging mud everywhere. They chased each other back and forth across their great new backyard. What fun! It seemed they played for hours.

"All this running and playing is making me hungry. Let's go get a snack." Sasha said to Erik. He was hungry too, and they raced each other to the doggy door. Just as they were about to squeeze through, Erik ran back into the yard and rolled his entire body in the red mud. "There," he thought, "much better."

Inside, still excited about their fun in the yard, they ran upstairs from the basement and chased each other around the house. Exhausted, they remembered the food bowls awaiting them. They ate and then they slept.

The sound of the garage door opening awakened the dogs. Andrea's car entered. Erik and Sasha got to their feet and made a path to the garage door to greet Andrea. They were excited to see her; she had been gone all day. They danced and twirled, howled their Samoyed howls, and waited.

Andrea opened the door, took one look and her mouth dropped open. "Oh, my beautiful white carpet! What have you two done? I can't believe what I'm seeing! What is this red, uh brown, uh red-brown stain all over my carpet? Oh! Oh! Oh!"

Erik could tell she wasn't happy. The two looked down to see why she was so upset. Sasha and Erik, for once, were in the doghouse together!

This was not pretty!

Andrea surveyed the damage, which was much worse downstairs where the two had tracked fresh mud. The sofa was circled by two sets of paw prints. Mud marks were everywhere – near the coffee table, in front of the fireplace, by the windows, and they made a path leading up the stairs.

"*Aarrggghhhh!!*" Andrea cried.

Erik and Sasha looked at one another. "This is not a good thing," Erik said. "Wait until Arthur gets home. He's going to be very disappointed. They may never let us inside the house again!" They both sighed and hung their heads and tails.

"I can't believe you've ruined my beautiful white carpet!" Andrea said to them, chasing them with towels intended to stop the damage from spreading. "I've got to get you clean and the worst of these stains up before Arthur gets home. You two just wait to see his face!"

Andrea started cleaning – with a vengeance. Erik and Sasha looked on, unable to do a thing to help her. "This is your fault!" Sasha whispered to Erik.

"How do you figure that, Miss Perfect Puppy? There's mud on your paws, too!" Erik responded.

"Well, you were the one who wanted to go out before the sun dried everything."

"I had to pee. It's not good to hold it."

"It isn't polite to use that word," Sasha corrected.

Erik kept the argument going. "This isn't about having to pee; it's about tracking mud on the carpet. Arthur always takes your side, but he may not this time. Look how angry Andrea is. He's not going to be happy with us either." Erik blew out a deep breath and waited, hiding behind an overstuffed chair in the living room.

"As if you think they can't see you." Sasha added with a huff. She always had to have the last word.

Arthur was due home any minute. Erik and Sasha didn't move, waiting to be scolded – again. They both wanted to run away, but decided to own up to their mischief.

Arthur walked into the house. He looked at Erik and Sasha and didn't say a word – not one word! "*Ooooohhhh*," thought the two of them. "This is definitely not good."

Erik and Sasha listened and watched as Andrea and Arthur walked through the house and talked about the damage to the carpet. They said they had no idea the clay would be so hard to deal with on the dogs' feet. They talked about the expense of ripping up their beautiful carpet and replacing it with tile. In the end, they agreed that white carpet, dog paws and Georgia clay do not mix.

Andrea said, "If we take away their freedom to come and go at will, we're setting ourselves up for inside accidents just like we had before. I don't want that. And one of the reasons we bought this home is so they could play in the yard anytime. This isn't their fault – it's ours for not predicting this would happen."

"Huh???" Erik and Sasha stared at each other. "We're not in trouble?"

Andrea saw them looking at one another and

knew immediately what they were thinking. "Oh no, you're not off the hook, you furry beasts. This mess of yours is going to take a lot of work to clean up. And, tile is expensive and we can't purchase it immediately. The two of you are going to have to use better judgment about where you go in the yard after a rain. In the meantime, *pleeeaaassse* stay on the grass and out of the mud when it rains!"

"They have no idea what you're saying," remarked Arthur with a roll of his eyes. But they did understand, and Andrea knew it.

A few weeks later, the white carpet was gone and replaced with Mexican tile, the exact color of the red clay of Georgia.

CHAPTER SIXTEEN

Andrea's new business was doing well and soon she needed to hire an assistant. Her office was in their home, so it was important that the new assistant love the dogs. The perfect person appeared, a woman named Kerri. She especially loved Erik, and she became his special companion when Andrea was away. Kerri also was an artist and often drew sketches of Erik as she talked on the phone.

One day, Kerri was doodling on a pad with the phone to her ear, with Erik sitting beside her. She drew a wonderful portrait of Erik, and showed it to him.

"Hey! That's me," Erik thought. It turned out to be such a good likeness that Kerri decided to frame it and give it to Andrea as a gift. It would become one of Andrea's prized possessions.

Time passed, and a man named Tim joined the office. He loved Erik immediately and whenever he had a few minutes of free time he would take Erik outside to play "catch."

Erik treasured the attention, but as he got older, he found it harder and harder to run fast enough to catch the ball. It was beginning to hurt his bones to go down the stairs that led out to the yard. Erik knew Tim's heart was good and he didn't want to disappoint him by appearing to be ungrateful for the exercise. He kept up as best as he could, but one day Tim noticed that Erik was slowing down.

A few weeks later, as Andrea and Erik were out for a walk around the neighborhood, Erik was having difficulty keeping her pace. "She has to hold back in order for me to walk beside her. Maybe I can convince her that I need a rest."

There was a special spot along their walk that was perfect for resting. That part of the neighborhood had a stream running through it. A cluster of Stone Mountain granite rocks were nestled beneath a huge old oak tree and they made the best sitting place. It was shady and the sounds of the stream nearby were very peaceful. "Let's go over here," Erik thought, as he pulled Andrea toward the rocks.

Sitting down on one of the large rocks, Andrea bent down to Erik and held his face to hers. "Tell me what's wrong, my beautiful friend."

Erik looked deep into her eyes. "I'm okay. I'm just having a little difficulty with my hips – nothing to worry about. I'll be fine." He tried to send that message as powerfully as he could, but Andrea knew that he was not fine.

At once, Erik's aging hit her. He had been by her side for seven years. She realized her precious friend would not be with her forever, and she shuddered at the thought of losing him. She felt as if her life was being torn apart.

They walked slowly back home.

A trip to the vet confirmed Andrea's fears. The doctor said Erik's hips were weak and aching, and recommended medicine for his pain. "The medicine will help him feel more comfortable," said the doctor, "but Erik's days of running and playing are over."

Andrea simply could not accept that. There had to be a better way.

Andrea had heard that there were veterinarians who offered treatments like those for humans with arthritis. These natural treatments built strength without doing harm, using the body's own energy to heal itself.

Andrea was relentless in her quest. Many phone calls later, she found the perfect doctor for Erik: Dr. Pat Zook. It turned out that Dr. Pat was a wonderful woman and a gifted, loving doctor.

Andrea and Arthur followed Dr. Pat's advice and under her supervision, Erik soon regained his energy and playfulness.

After just a few visits to Dr. Pat, Erik grew strong enough that Andrea and Arthur took him and Sasha on a vacation to the beaches of Oregon. "What fun it is to run and play like a young dog again!" Erik thought. "I can even out run that Sasha!"

Erik taught Sasha the tricks he had once played with the ocean waves in Charleston. She loved it, and the game was more fun for Erik now with two dogs challenging each other to see who could stay dry the longest. They even found a stray crab trying to make its way back to the safety of the ocean and helped it along by barking and nudging it with their noses.

It was a happy time once again and easy for Andrea to slip into the false, yet comforting, belief that Erik would remain forever young.

•

Over time, Erik found himself being drawn to the wooded backyard at his home. There was a special place he liked to sit and just be quiet. He often thought of the Princess there.

"You would have liked this place, Princess. You and I never had so much space to roam around in the yard before. And there are all kinds of animals that sneak inside the fence from time to time. Even you would love to chase them!"

In those quietest of moments, he found he could easily connect with his old friend, the Princess. He didn't have to howl or make dog sounds to get her attention – all he had to do was think about communicating with her, and she would very gently enter his mind.

Erik sensed her response to him. "I know, my friend. It is a beautiful place with grass and trees, flowering bushes, and even a little red clay that can get you into trouble if you're not careful." He chuckled at her comment about the clay and knew she was teasing him.

Sometimes, when his bones would ache and he wouldn't dare allow Andrea to know he was hurting, he would ask, "What's happening to me, Princess? Am I going to die, like you did?"

The Princess glanced at White Wolf, whose

presence she could sense at all times, for the answer. White Wolf said, "Not yet, Princess. He's not ready."

She didn't answer Erik's question directly; instead, she sent him love. But Erik thought he knew the answer, and he was afraid.

REFLECTIONS
Appreciating What Is

In the heart-wrenching poem "The Fourth Day," Martin Scot Kosins describes three days in an animal companion's life that his or her person will always remember. The first day is that joyful time an animal friend comes into your life. The third day is that awful and inevitable instant your friend leaves you and, as Kosins says, you "feel as alone as a single star in the dark night." The middle day is marked by a moment of observation and followed by a passage of time. It begins when you suddenly realize your friend is no longer a carefree youth but rather an aging soul – old bones and slower footsteps. Like Andrea did, you might feel a deep pang of fear, dreading what lies ahead, realizing the time is finite.

There is profound beauty in this realization if one stays present. Whether it involves an aging animal companion or a beloved human, it is literally a wake-up call. Heeding the call does not mean suffering in anticipation of loss. Quite the contrary; it offers the opportunity to fully engage in the experience of accepting and even appreciating what is, awakening and cherishing the new phase in your life together.

Why do dogs have such brief lives compared with humans? Perhaps their short life expectancy is another gift that teaches us to treasure each experience. It's easy for parents to take their children for granted. Life's chores don't often allow for time to lie in the grass with them and decipher cloud animals. Those children rapidly become busy teenagers who themselves have neither time nor patience for the stories of the wise great-grandmother. The irony is significant. So many of us fear what we consider big losses like death, yet we throw away precious experiences as if they are as worthless as a candy wrapper.

Seizing the moment can co-exist with life's realities and responsibilities. It does represent a significant trade-off, though not so much of tasks and to-do's. To fully appreciate the downy feel of soft fur, the sweet smell of a baby's neck or the wisdom of an elder's eyes, we choose to trade mental clutter and the flotsam and jetsam of our thoughts, worries and obsessions, for the experience at hand. The to-do list in your mind can be retrieved, the worries revisited later – that is, they can be retrieved if they have not been transformed by the sights, sounds and smells of the present moment.

That moment can change everything.

When Andrea's dad was ill, his sister and her husband used the occasions of his frequent doctor visits to spend time with him. They would pick him up from his home, drive him to the doctor in a neighboring city, then take him out to lunch or dinner afterwards. It was a welcome break for his wife, Andrea's mother, as it was one less chore for her, and he enjoyed the company. If Andrea happened to be home from college on a break, she would accompany them.

Andrea enjoyed these outings immensely, though she secretly felt guilty about the enjoyment. It seemed as if they were out celebrating, using his illness as a reason to connect with relatives and take pleasure in a meal. This period of time was like the second day. While anyone would have wished for another reason to enjoy a visit, he was, in fact, terminally ill. Making the most of the time they had together was both an acceptance of reality and an appreciation – even celebration – of precious time. To despair over what was to come (at some future date no one could predict) would have eclipsed the aliveness of the moment.

Many years later, Andrea's guilt was transformed as she learned this lesson from an aging Erik.

What precious thing in your life is calling for your attention right now?

"To everything there is a season,
And a time to every purpose under heaven."

Ecclesiastes 3:1

CHAPTER SEVENTEEN

For nearly three years after the first visit to Dr. Pat, Erik lived comfortably. Erik and Andrea had become very close through the years, but now they were inseparable companions. Whenever possible, he went where she went. When Erik's aching hips didn't allow him to take long walks, Andrea took him out to lunch with her. They sat alone together at dog-friendly restaurants, enjoying the sights and sounds, but most of all, treasuring each other's company.

After lunch they often window-shopped, taking their time to talk with friendly people who stopped to pet Erik and tell him how beautiful he was. During this time, Andrea noticed that something magical was happening – they were communicating without the need for words.

When Erik realized that Andrea was finally aware of their non-verbal communication, he thought to himself, "Well, it sure took her long enough to figure this little trick out. We could have saved ourselves a lot of time and energy by communicating this way a long time ago." He thought about how he had learned to talk to White Wolf and the Princess without using human words, and was glad to be able to finally connect with Andrea in this way.

Eventually, Erik was again finding it difficult to walk without pain. Dr. Pat was still working her healing magic and after every visit, he would recover for a while. But it was obvious his body was becoming more fragile with each passing day.

Sasha, who was still a young dog, would try to get him to play. "Sasha, I need to rest," he tried to tell her. But she was relentless, and sometimes he had to growl to get the message through to her.

•

One day, Andrea received a call from a good friend. Mary Ann excitedly told Andrea about a wonderful trip she and her husband were planning and invited Andrea and Arthur to come along. The trip was to Italy – a dream vacation to a place they'd always longed to visit. Immediately, Andrea was torn between the thrill of the trip and the fear of leaving Erik behind. They would be away for two weeks, and though Erik was getting by just fine, Andrea wanted to be there if he needed her. Time with him was precious.

That night, Arthur and Andrea discussed the trip. They decided they would go on one condition: that the dogs' "grandma" (Andrea's mother) would care for them while they were away. She would nurture Erik and Sasha with the love and attention they got at home. Grandma agreed, and they made plans to drive the dogs from Atlanta to her home in Illinois.

The night before the trip to Illinois, Andrea said to Arthur, "I'm very excited about our vacation in Italy, but I just can't help but worry. What if Erik gets sick or falls down the steps at my mother's house? I'm afraid to leave him." Arthur tried to ease her mind, but when she went to bed that night she couldn't sleep.

Andrea rolled and tossed, and finally gave up on sleep. She got up, called Erik to her, and went to her office. They sat on the sofa together. Andrea said to Erik:

"Big Dog, you probably don't understand a word of this, but I have to say it. Tomorrow we are taking you to Grandma's house to stay for two weeks. She's the one who feeds you eggs and bacon and has squirrels in her yard that are so tame you can almost catch them. I know you like visiting there, but I fear you will miss me and think I've abandoned you. Please know I love you mightily, with all my heart, and that I'll be back in no time. And Erik . . . " She paused and forced back tears. "You must promise me you will wait for me."

Erik looked into her eyes and sent love. He promised, though he didn't know how to tell her so. He could feel White Wolf's presence in the corner of the room, watching them. He thought that perhaps Andrea was feeling him too, because she glanced that way several times, and she seemed to relax more and more. They went back to bed.

In the wee hours of that night, Andrea had the most remarkable dream. In it, Erik came to her. She was clear that the dog in her dream was Erik, except that he was a hologram. She relayed the dream to Arthur the next morning.

"Nothing really 'happened' and there was no dialogue between us. He just appeared to me, much like Princess Leia calling on Obi Wan Kenobi in the Star Wars film. I heard music too – I'm sure of that. I can't recall it; I just know that it was comforting. What's remarkable is that, all at once, I had a realization that Erik and I are inseparable. He is everywhere I am

– a part of me really – and being in Europe doesn't distance us. I have complete peace about the trip. I'm ready to go."

Arthur smiled. He didn't want to discourage Andrea, though he thought her dream was a bit far-fetched.

REFLECTIONS
Infinite Connection

Andrea's dream of the hologram had impact beyond reassurance for the trip to Italy. While she would not have been able to articulate this at the time, she was given a glimpse of infinity, a new awareness of the nature of consciousness and the nature of space and time. It was simply a manifestation of a higher truth Andrea understood on a level not accessible while awake. And it built a foundation for her faith that the soul survives physical death, faith that would be tested later when Erik did eventually die.

" . . . the purpose of life is to learn. We are indeed on a shaman's journey, mere children struggling to become technicians of the sacred . . . As long as the formlessness and breathtaking freedom of the beyond remain frightening to us, we will continue to dream a hologram for ourselves that is comfortably solid and well defined . . . We are, as the aborigines say, just learning to survive in infinity."

Michael Talbot

The Holographic Universe
1991 HarperCollins Publishers

CHAPTER EIGHTEEN

Andrea and Arthur returned from Italy to find their beloved dogs healthy and happy. The visit to Grandma's house had been good for them. Andrea thought that perhaps Erik had even gained a pound or two – no doubt from eating bacon and eggs each morning. That was a good thing, as Dr. Pat always encouraged Andrea to try to get more weight on Erik. Sasha, however, had the opposite problem and was promptly put on a diet.

The family drove back home to Atlanta and life was normal for a short time after that.

Slowly, others close to the family began noticing Erik's condition worsening. Tim saw how hard it was for Erik to go up and down the steps from the deck to the backyard. He loved Erik and wanted to spare him the pain. He found some scrap wood in the garage and built a ramp so Erik wouldn't have to hurt his hips using the steps. He still threw the ball for Erik each day, but not quite as far or as fast as he had in the past.

Erik appreciated everyone's efforts to make life more comfortable for him, yet it seemed he wanted and needed more time alone. Once outside, he headed for the heavily wooded section of the backyard. He spent even more time there now. It was his special place to think, and talk with his old friend the Princess.

One night, Erik was in his usual spot in the backyard. As he looked around, he hoped mightily he would be able to hear the Princess' wise voice in his head. He had many questions. While he knew his body was deteriorating rapidly, he wasn't ready to go. He wanted to go on living here with this family he loved so much – especially with Andrea, his friend and student. "I still have much to teach her, and she needs me." There were so many questions Erik couldn't answer. "How will Andrea manage without me?"

As Erik tried to connect with the Princess, he realized he missed her more now than ever. She would understand what he was going through because she had experienced it with Arthur. She had shared her feelings with Erik during those last days and he needed her now to remind him. Sasha was still too young to help him through this time.

He was trying too hard to connect and it wasn't working. He had to still his mind. He breathed deeply and focused.

Gazing toward the stars in the night sky, Erik asked in desperation, "Is leaving always this hard?"

Instantly he sensed a wise and loving presence. It was the Princess! "She hasn't abandoned me. I'm connecting with her – speaking with her – right here in the woods!" All he had to do was calm his thoughts and reach out to her and she was there for him.

Years before she had promised she would be there when it was his time to go, and she was keeping her word. This time though, Erik experienced something new. He could actually see a faint image of the Princess in the trees. She was surrounded by the most beautiful light and he felt intense love radiating in all directions. There was a second, much larger light by her side – his teacher, White Wolf. This comforted him and he asked his question. "Princess, my body says it's time to go. I hurt and I no longer enjoy the things a dog takes for granted – walks, good food, and even hugs and kisses from my family. But my heart tells me I must stay."

The Princess understood his struggle and felt

deep compassion for him. While she had vast wisdom available to her now, she could only send him love. She knew that he would soon understand what she understood so well. Erik would have to leave his aged body behind – but he would not have to leave his precious Andrea and his connection to her heart.

White Wolf spoke to the Princess, "Erik is almost ready. I will begin to prepare him."

CHAPTER NINETEEN

It was a beautiful summer in Georgia and one day Andrea and Arthur had friends over to visit. Usually Erik loved company, but like all the other things he loved, these days he had little energy for friends.

As the group were enjoying their afternoon conversation, Arthur suddenly had a strange feeling. "Where's Erik?" he asked Andrea.

"Probably resting," she said. Then, noticing the funny look on Arthur's face, she got up to check. Panicked, she saw the front door wide open. Erik was nowhere to be found.

Arthur ran out of the house, frantically calling for him. Even though his street days were long in the past, Erik had kept his nomadic instincts. No one knew how long the door had been open and Arthur worried that Erik was in trouble. Andrea stayed with the guests while Arthur began searching the neighborhood.

Arthur reluctantly approached the creek behind their house. He feared the worst. As he reached the edge, he could see Erik standing in the middle of the creek, covered with red silt. Arthur called to him and Erik seemed dazed and confused. Arthur waded into the muddy creek, picked Erik up and tearfully carried him home. To Arthur, this was a sign Erik was fading away. He didn't even seem to recognize the family he had loved so much.

As Andrea saw them approach the house, she was both relieved that Erik was safe and terrified at the thought that he could have drowned. Once in the house, she wrapped Erik in towels and gently cleaned his fur. Arthur seemed very upset, but Andrea brushed aside his fears by teasing Erik about running away and once again getting covered in red clay.

Arthur was as worried about Andrea as he was about Erik. "She's pretending this isn't happening," he thought. But she knew what was happening. She just didn't know how to talk about it. The incident at the creek was another example – a dangerous one for sure – of the increasing amount of time Erik was spending alone, outdoors, seemingly disconnected from the world around him.

Often Andrea and Arthur would watch from the kitchen window as Erik stood still as a statue, looking toward the sky. At night, he would go to his favorite spot and stare at the stars. Erik could feel the forces of nature. His instincts were calling him back to the wild . . . and to a time before he was on the earth.

Neither Andrea nor Arthur could understand what he was doing. Dr. Pat explained this was Erik's way of transitioning from his physical body. She said, "Erik's connecting with his element, his essence or spirit. It's a natural and beautiful way of preparing to leave the earth."

Still, it was confusing. "Why," thought Andrea, "would our loving friend leave us to be outside alone when time with us is so precious?"

This time of transition for Erik was a painful time for the humans.

•

"White Wolf, I had a dream last night," Erik began. "Well, I don't know if it was a dream or not, because I wasn't exactly sleeping. I was standing at the edge of the woods in our yard."

"Tell me more, Erik."

"At first I felt the immense love that accompanies your presence. But then it became so strong that it lifted me . . . uh, actually I became it. Yes, I became the love itself and, all of a sudden, I felt a part of everyone and everything. I was at once the trees, the crickets, the soil . . . and Andrea! I remember feeling Andrea; she was vast and powerful. I was her, the real her . . . and then you, and then . . . All That Is."

White Wolf spoke. "Erik, you and Andrea, and all living things, are a part of All That Is. We are all connected, inseparable and perfect. Bodies may age and hurt, the trees may rot and fall, but the wholeness will return. Soon you will fully know this circle of life."

•

Even though Andrea had outwardly dismissed the creek incident, Arthur noticed that she now tried to keep Erik at her side as much as possible. Her loving hand was never far from his body. Arthur watched as she made choices he had never seen her make before – some days she rearranged business appointments to attend to Erik's needs, including trips to see Dr. Pat.

Erik was proud of Andrea too, not for his sake but for hers – she was learning to listen to her heart.

One evening Erik became very sick. During that long night, Andrea held Erik in her arms for hours, fearing perhaps the end was near and he would leave her soon.

The next morning she canceled a business meeting to take him to see Dr. Pat. At 7:00 a.m., she called her client and said, "I won't be able to make the meeting because Erik is very sick and I must take him to the vet." This was a surprise to Andrea's client and he didn't know how to react. He said he was disappointed and didn't understand.

Andrea had to make a choice. She had opened her heart to Erik, and her commitment to him was the most important thing to her that morning.

As it turned out, Erik recovered from his setback. His work was not yet done. Andrea knew there would be more times when she would have to reschedule appointments because Erik needed her. She always took care of commitments she'd made to her clients and her work didn't suffer. Yet the change in Andrea was strange to those around her – some understood and accepted her new way of being; others did not.

Andrea had always been poised and had perfected the art of self-control. Her business clients knew her as a very good listener, someone who cared about them and their needs. Before Erik's aging and illness, she didn't allow anyone else to know her feelings, at least not when she was feeling scared or sad. Now, she was slowly learning to share her thoughts and fears with others, and she was making choices that were very different from those she'd made in earlier years.

Andrea needed friends to lean on like never before. She tried to reason with herself, at the same time attempting to access her own intuition. This reasoning made it impossible for her to even hear her inner wisdom. Her pain was getting in the way. She was torn between knowing that the right thing to do was to let Erik go, and knowing the sadness and pain that would come from being without him.

One morning in early August, Andrea was trying to wrap up her work in order to leave and meet a client for a lunch. She was running behind, not able to concentrate on simple tasks. To make matters worse, she was distracted by a song playing in her head – a song she had always loved. This day, though, it made her anxious and sad, and she tried to push it from her mind. As is so often the case, the harder she tried, the louder it became. The repeated refrain of "Landslide" seemed to insist that she face her fears.

At lunch, she could not shake the anxiety. Her client, Elizabeth, was quickly becoming a friend and recognized that Andrea was not herself. She asked,

"What's making you feel sad, Andrea? You're usually so positive and strong, but today you don't look well."

Andrea replied, "I don't know what to do about Erik. I fear he's hurting and that I should let him go, but it's so hard for me to lose him. I've been through many changes in my life and I weather them well. This one is overwhelming. I can't imagine life without him."

Elizabeth looked upward and paused as if she were praying. Her reply to Andrea was: "He said you know what to do."

At that moment, Andrea realized that she did know, and that it was time for Erik to leave the earth. But how?

CHAPTER TWENTY

Though Erik was old and very sick, he felt proud that Andrea was learning every day. That made him happy. Still, she was just beginning to really feel love and joy, and he knew she was also in great emotional pain. Erik had no way of knowing that the most important lessons she would learn would come with his death; Andrea would learn to feel at the deepest level, and express her grief and loss.

On the evening of Andrea's lunch with Elizabeth, Erik stood, once again, in the corner of the backyard under the stars.

"I can't do it. I just can't go yet." Erik argued with himself.

White Wolf appeared as if in response to Erik's plea.

"I don't think I can bear the pain of leaving Andrea and Arthur. I know I'm going to a place where I will be healed and whole, but they will be left behind in their human bodies and will ache for me."

Erik now completely understood the importance of what the Princess had meant when she had asked him to take care of Arthur. "But who will take care of Andrea?"

"My friend, in these past weeks you have had glimpses of the awesome connectedness that exists among all things, even after death. Still, I know you are struggling with leaving this earth and your family." White Wolf conveyed deep empathy.

Erik felt White Wolf's compassion. It was as though he were a real being who had wrapped Erik in soft, warm light. He hoped White Wolf could understand his questions. "I know what's in Andrea's heart and mind. I can feel her sadness and, at the same time, I know she doesn't want me to suffer in pain."

Erik knew that Andrea felt terrified of losing him, even as she watched his physical body slip away, bit by bit, hour by hour. While he loved her so, he hoped she would soon know what to do. He surely didn't.

He asked in earnest, "White Wolf, what can I do?"

The message he received from White Wolf was

simple, "Just tell her."

Late that night, Andrea and Erik were sitting on the floor of the bedroom, a room where Erik had been spending most of his time while in the house. Andrea placed her face close to Erik's and asked, "Do you hurt, precious friend?"

He looked up into her eyes and sent the most powerful message he was capable of sending. It had been months since the usually very vocal Erik had uttered a sound. But at that moment he replied with a soft, yet crystal clear sound. "Yes," his gentle howl conveyed.

In that moment, Andrea knew that Erik had given her the permission she needed. She sank her face into his beautiful white fur, as she did so often these days, and tearfully told him she understood.

The next morning, she picked up the phone and called Dr. Pat.

•

As Erik, Andrea, and Arthur waited for Dr. Pat to arrive, Andrea and Erik took a slow walk to the wooded area in the backyard. They stood together in his favorite spot.

Andrea told Erik, "I love you with all my heart

and in ways I can't explain. You are my best friend, my patient teacher, my wonderful companion. You love me unconditionally even when I'm not my best person. I thank you – for all you have given me."

Her words choked. She sank to her knees and covered Erik with kisses and tears. Then, she carried Erik into the house and laid him on the sofa. He ate very little these days, but she was able to feed him bits of crackers until Dr. Pat arrived. He liked that, and for a brief moment they both imagined he was young and healthy once again.

Erik was thankful to see Dr. Pat. He had grown to love her and knew she was there to help him make the passing easier. "I hope Dr. Pat will be able to explain to Andrea that everything will be okay for both of us."

Dr. Pat sat on the floor with Erik, Andrea, and Arthur, and she spoke with loving compassion, "Sometimes our animal friends struggle to stay alive for us, because we can't let them go. I've learned that often an animal is more at peace once the human decides to let him go. Even though Erik doesn't want to leave you, his spirit will be with you, everywhere, all of the time. Some of them are master teachers. Erik is one of these special ones. It's okay to let him go."

Then, Dr. Pat spoke directly to Erik. "I know you don't want to go, but you can come right back. This body just won't work anymore. You can come right back. You didn't do anything wrong, it's just time to go . . . this time."

Dr. Pat sensed Erik still didn't want to leave, so she consoled him by saying, "If you want to be with these people again, come back."

Erik understood, and, with a gentle Samoyed howl, turned his head toward Andrea and sent his message.

"I love you. I will be back."

And then he was gone.

ERIK'S HOPE
THE LEASH THAT LED ME TO FREEDOM

PART II

CHAPTER TWENTY-ONE

Andrea felt a rush of energy move past her right shoulder, and then – nothing. Erik was gone.

The skies turned dark and rain pelted the windows. Thunder began to shake the house. Andrea turned to Dr. Pat and asked, "Now what do I do?"

•

"White Wolf, where am I?" Erik asked. He spoke softly at first and then became more excited. "And how did I get here – where is my body? I feel so light, so free like I could fly. There's no pain in my hips – I don't even know where my hips are!"

"Erik, you are part of All That Is," White Wolf replied. "You are truly free to be anywhere and everywhere. Look around."

"Oh, White Wolf, it's all so beautiful. I see grass greener than I could ever imagine. And the light . . . it's bright and warm and . . . White Wolf, where is Andrea?"

"She is there Erik. Just focus and you will see her."

"Oh, no!" Erik exclaimed. "She's crying. Why is she crying? Is Andrea sick? What's the matter with her?"

Calmly, White Wolf responded, "Andrea is grieving, Erik. She feels very sad that you're not there with her. She can't stroke your fur or gaze into your beautiful eyes. But, this is an important time for Andrea. As difficult as physical death is for humans, it's part of the circle of life. Andrea's special bond with you paves the way for her to understand that time with others on earth is a gift, yet spirit lives on."

"Watching her cry makes me sad, White Wolf. Does she think I no longer love her?"

"Not exactly, Erik," White Wolf explained. "The love you two have for one another will never end. Yet Andrea must accept the fact that you're no longer with her as her Erik, her sweet Samoyed friend she talked with each day and cuddled with each night. Your entire life with Andrea prepared her for this moment.

She learned, through your work with her, how to feel all the things humans feel when they are at their best. She learned what is really important in the life of a human being – being loved and giving love. You and I know that this kind of love doesn't die. Ever! Now, Andrea is getting a test – you could call it a test of her faith, her faith that the love you shared was real."

"Of course it was real, White Wolf," Erik said. "I'll just send her love now, the way you did for me when I was a dog on earth."

"Erik, you do have the ability to send her love and connect your spirit to hers, just like I did with you. But you must not do this now. If you go to her too soon, it will interfere. We must let Andrea experience the feelings she has, even though they're very painful. It's part of being human. And you, my friend, must rest. You must prepare for your next journey, a very important one."

"My next journey? I don't understand, White Wolf. I don't want to go anywhere if I won't be with Andrea!"

"You will be with her Erik. I promise you that. Now rest, dear soul."

CHAPTER TWENTY-TWO

White Wolf remained to observe the scene unfold with Andrea, Arthur and Dr. Pat. He knew the feelings Andrea would soon experience and wondered what choices she would make. He decided to call on a friend.

"Princess? Hello Princess, please come to me." Soon White Wolf was joined by the Princess, who had been watching Erik and Andrea closely in the past days.

Since her death years prior, the Princess had been waiting patiently, watching over the pair as Andrea grew and Erik worked toward fulfilling his mission in her life. There had been so many times she had wanted to step in, touch Andrea with a loving paw and tell her that all would work out, but she knew she mustn't interfere. She was happy that Erik was able to sense her love, and gratified that he called upon her wisdom in his last months on earth.

White Wolf greeted the Princess and then he spoke. "This is the time we have been anticipating. It will be at once a joy to observe and also very difficult to watch, as Andrea completes this major step in her life on earth."

White Wolf began to explain, "Prior to Erik's death, Andrea had to make a difficult decision, one she would like to have avoided. She didn't want to choose between ending Erik's life and allowing him to continue to live with a rapidly failing body and mind. The decision to finally let him go had been much harder for her than she anticipated. Even though Andrea didn't know how she was going to live without her best friend, she believed that life on earth was not the end for either of them. This belief was comforting, and was the reason she was able to summon the courage to let him go."

"But she has been naïve. She now expects to sense Erik, to feel his spirit with her all the time. We've decided not to let this happen for awhile, as Andrea must learn to feel the pain of separation, the pain of loss. She will experience raw grief. No human can escape this lesson. But we'll make it as comfortable as possible."

"White Wolf, how can we help? How can we make it more comfortable?" asked the Princess.

"Watch and you'll see, Princess," White Wolf responded. "There are many gifts and blessings available to Andrea at this time; we've arranged that. She, like every human, has free will. That means she alone gets to choose what to do with these gifts. I believe that Andrea will allow her friends and family to show her love, care, and support in ways that she's never experienced before. Her heart is open wide because of the unconditional love that Erik gave her. Even though she will have doubts over the next few days and weeks, deep inside, Andrea knows that his love was real and that it does not die. That belief, that faith, will give her the courage and strength she needs to get through the sadness of losing Erik physically."

"How, White Wolf?" the Princess asked.

"Princess, when humans accept that they are worthy of unconditional love and open their hearts to receive that love, they often find treasures buried, waiting all along to be discovered. Andrea's treasures will come in the form of simple acts of kindness and compassion that people will show her."

"That sounds like what dogs do," said the Princess. "When I was on earth, my special person was Arthur.

I knew that he loved me very much, with all his heart. I was happy anywhere, doing anything, as long as I was with him. When I got older and had less energy, Arthur took me to the lake at a nearby park every weekend. We sat on the ground together by the water and watched ducks splashing. They made quite a commotion. As we sat, Arthur brushed my fur coat until it glistened in the sun."

"Do you think Arthur will take Andrea to the park, White Wolf?" Princess asked.

"I don't know, Princess. I do know that he'll help her very much in the coming days, even though he, too, is very sad that Erik is no longer part of the family. Let's observe for awhile," White Wolf suggested.

White Wolf and the Princess settled in to watch the Chilcotes begin to make their way through their grief.

CHAPTER TWENTY-THREE

Dr. Pat, thinking that Andrea's question "Now what do I do?" was an immediate and practical one, began taking charge.

She responded, "I know some kind people who can come and help us. They provide funeral services for animals. I'll call and arrange for them to come right away."

This wasn't the question Andrea had in mind, but she knew she had to take care of this detail. Wringing her hands and with eyes glued to the floor, she collapsed on the sofa as Dr. Pat picked up the phone. Dr. Pat was an angel.

Two men arrived shortly at Andrea's and Arthur's home. Dr. Pat guided them into the room where Erik's body lay still on the sofa. They had brought a stretcher made up like a bed with white sheets. With care and compassion, the men lifted Erik's body onto the stretcher and slowly covered him with the sheet. The whole surreal scene was set to the music of Elton John's "Love Songs" compilation album, which had been playing repeatedly for hours.

Andrea watched the process, certain that Erik was no longer there. Erik's body was just a shell for the precious soul she loved so very much. As the men left, Andrea was glad this part was over.

Andrea still hoped that she would feel Erik's presence, feel him return in some small way. No matter how hard she concentrated, he wasn't there. The music that had so comforted her just moments before suddenly became irritating. Just as the refrain from "Can You Feel the Love Tonight?" began, she clicked off the stereo. It would be some time before she summoned the courage to play that CD again.

The clock ticked away. Andrea paced the floor in the main part of the house. She stared down at the Saltillo tiles, the very tile the family had installed to replace the mud-ruined carpet so many years before. She thought that she would never feel the same joy in her life again, the joy of those days when Erik was a rambunctious and sometimes mischievous youngster. Her thoughts were interrupted by a sound coming from a nearby room. It was Arthur.

•

"White Wolf, do something!" Princess exclaimed. "Arthur is crying. Oh, please, White Wolf. It hurts me to see him – both of them – so sad!"

"Princess, just watch what happens next," White Wolf responded gently to her pleas.

•

Andrea forgot about her own grief for just a moment as she heard Arthur's sobs. She walked toward him, passing by the large window that framed the wooded area of their yard. The rain had stopped suddenly, though only temporarily. But for this brief moment, the sun peeked through the clouds, creating over the trees the first of many gifts that Andrea would be offered in the coming days.

"Arthur! Arthur, come quickly!" Andrea exclaimed.

Not hearing footsteps, Andrea ran to Arthur and embraced him briefly before leading him by the hand, first to the window then out the door onto the deck.

"Look," Andrea said softly.

Arthur saw the rainbow. The two of them stood

watching it, arm in arm, for several minutes. Then, as suddenly as it had appeared, the rainbow vanished. The rain began again, torrential rain that would continue for hours. They went inside. Andrea knew that Erik's transition from physical body to spiritual body was complete.

Erik was watching. He recalled White Wolf's counsel earlier, and thought to himself, "Andrea, I'm not far away, but I must leave you to your journey. I'll come back to you when you're ready. I promise that, and I hope it's soon."

•

For the next hour, Andrea's tears poured like the rain outside. Then, suddenly, she took a deep breath, got up from her chair and went upstairs. She found a soft cloth, soaked it with cool water and placed it over her face to ease the swelling in her eyes. As Andrea looked steadily in the mirror, the feelings began rushing back. She moved away before the tears could follow. It was time to attend to a task that she had been dreading, telling her friends and family that Erik was gone.

Andrea's friends had loved Erik too, and the closest of them had known this day was imminent.

Holding her breath, Andrea picked up the phone and dialed Art and Mary Ann, the friends she and Arthur had traveled with to Italy. That call and the ones that followed got her through the next few hours. Little did Andrea know they would set the stage for a life-altering choice.

Andrea had many friends, people with whom she enjoyed spending time. She was generous and caring toward her friends, and people liked being around her. She inspired them; she was the kind of person that made people feel good about themselves.

No one except Arthur knew the part of Andrea that needed the very thing she gave so freely to others. It was as if she wore a protective shell, and tears certainly couldn't penetrate the shell. At least not until the day Erik left.

The conversation with Art was a blur. Andrea choked on her words from the very start of the call and that made Art cry, too. When she hung up the phone, she thought, "That was a disaster. I'm clearly not very good at this."

She went upstairs to her office and sat down at her computer, thinking that email might be an easier way of telling everyone that Erik had passed away.

Sitting at her desk, Andrea immediately felt distracted. She got up and walked toward the closet where she pulled out a large brown box. The box was bulging and even splitting in places from its heavy contents. It contained photographs, unorganized, unsorted, heaped into the box as the years had piled up. Andrea began searching for photos of Erik and the tears began again. She let them fall freely onto the old box flaps, giving the room a faint wet musty smell.

Absorbed in her work and the emotion that accompanied it, Andrea was startled by the 'ding' indicating new email. She got up to check.

The email was from Art. In the time that had passed since the call, he had written a poem for Andrea, a sweet poem that memorialized Erik's life. Reading the passage, Andrea knew Art understood how important Erik's relationship was to her, and that he realized, as did she, that losing an animal friend was just as significant as losing a human friend. She cherished this gesture and it gave her the courage to make more phone calls.

CHAPTER TWENTY-FOUR

"White Wolf, can I visit Erik?" the Princess asked. "I'm just bursting with excitement about seeing him here."

"I think he would like that, Princess." White Wolf responded. "Don't stay too long though. We must let him get his rest. Remember what I told you we were planning for Erik," White Wolf added with a wink.

"Oh yes, I remember," the Princess said, eyes twinkling with delight for her friend, Erik.

Soon Erik and the Princess were joyfully reunited. After they caught up a bit, they decided to watch Andrea.

"Princess, I wish we could visit Andrea. Don't you think we should help her?" Erik asked.

"Oh Erik, we can help her more from here. In

fact, I have an idea."

"What?" Erik asked.

"Well, I know White Wolf wants us to leave Andrea alone. But he didn't say anything about Arthur . . . " She smiled slyly and Erik nodded, getting a sense of what the Princess was up to.

•

While Andrea was absorbed in her project with the old photographs, Arthur made his way to the living room sofa and promptly fell into a deep sleep. He dreamed.

In his dream, Arthur found himself in his and Andrea's favorite Atlanta restaurant, a classic Italian eatery called Gino's. He was seated alone, drinking a glass of red wine. Then as dreams often do, Arthur's took an unusual twist. The Maitre d' walked toward Arthur and spoke in his heavy Italian accent.

"Mr. Chilcote?"

"Yes sir?" Arthur replied, looking up from his menu.

"There is someone here who would like to join you," Mario said.

At first Arthur saw only Mario. Then looking down, he saw – could it be? The Princess!

Since there are no rules of etiquette in dreams, Arthur jumped to his feet, knocking over his wine glass. His napkin fell to the floor as he embraced the Princess. Just as he felt her soft fur, he heard a sound, a word. "Celebrate," the voice said. And then the Princess was gone and Arthur awoke with a start.

•

"Andrea?" Arthur called up the stairs. "Andrea, what are you doing?"

Not getting a response, Arthur climbed the stairs. He walked toward Andrea's office and found her sitting on the floor with her back to the doorway. She seemed to be sorting through old photographs.

"Andrea?"

Andrea was startled by Arthur's presence and jumped. He apologized and they embraced. Arthur spoke.

"I have an idea," he said cautiously.

"What?"

"I think we should go out to dinner tonight, go to Gino's. Get all dressed up, have champagne, and celebrate Erik's life, and how fortunate we are to have had such a wonderful dog share our lives for ten years."

Arthur held his breath as he watched Andrea's face for a response. She began to smile, then nodded the "yes" response he had been waiting for. A tear rolled down her cheek but the smile remained.

"Great idea, Arthur," she said, and then Arthur smiled too.

•

"Great idea, Princess," said Erik. "She smiled." The two dog spirits exchanged smiles too.

•

So that Saturday evening Andrea and Arthur drove into Atlanta to Gino's, their favorite Italian restaurant, to celebrate Erik's life and his many gifts to them. As they drove, Andrea tried turning her thoughts to celebration instead of her emptiness. It was very hard to concentrate and she worried that this might not have been a good idea after all.

Arriving at Gino's, Andrea and Arthur were greeted with the usual friendly welcoming from the owner. They were seated at their favorite table and ordered a bottle of champagne. All seemed to be going well.

Andrea and Arthur talked about Erik's many runaways and how frightened they'd been until they found him. They laughed in their remembrance of coming home and finding the blinds demolished in his attempt to get their attention. Andrea revisited the delight of the sand dollar discovery on the beach with her best friend.

They found joy in remembering Erik's and the Princess' closeness as their relationship had matured, and they commented on how humanlike the animals' actions had been. Erik had had a wonderful life and they loved him for his contributions to their own.

Neither got through the conversation without shedding tears and the server began to notice something was wrong as he took their order. Andrea selected spaghetti – always a favorite, and Arthur ordered only an appetizer.

Waiting for the food to arrive at their table, Arthur made a toast to Erik P. Chilcote. It was short – it was sweet. He couldn't manage anything more at the time.

Eventually their beautifully presented dinner appeared. With the break in conversation brought on by the arrival of the food, Andrea became overwhelmed by the void of Erik's presence. Her tears began to flow, spilling onto the plate of spaghetti. Red sauce splattered her blouse as the droplets hit the plate and formed little craters.

The staff, who had known Andrea and Arthur for several years, became very anxious about the couple and notified the owner of the Chilcotes' distress. Mario quickly approached their table.

"I don't mean to intrude," he said, "but you look as though something is very wrong. What can I do to help you? You both appear so pained."

Andrea couldn't talk.

Arthur explained, "We lost Erik this morning, Mario. And we thought that celebrating his life would help ease the sadness of his passing."

Mario remembered Erik with fondness. Andrea would sometimes have Erik with her when she had short errands in the city and would drop by the restaurant on her way home to pick up their favorite Italian dishes for dinner. While she and Erik waited for the order to come, Mario would treat Erik to wonderful buttery garlic rolls. Erik would eat the rolls, then lick the dripping butter from Mario's fingers. Mario smiled at the memory.

Mario knelt between them at the table. He reached up and took Arthur's left hand and Andrea's right into his own. "I know your pain is great, and it will be a long time before those huge holes in your hearts fill again. Try to find some comfort in knowing that all of us who knew Erik, loved him. And we love you." He gently squeezed their hands in his, then left the table, tears welling in his own eyes as he walked away.

Andrea and Arthur were silent for the remainder of the meal. The drive home was equally as silent. There was no more energy for talking.

At home, exhausted with the emotion of the day, they crawled into bed. Andrea hoped with all her might that she might feel something, dream something to allow her some kind of communication with Erik. Instead she slept soundly and without dreams.

CHAPTER TWENTY-FIVE

On Sunday morning, Andrea awoke with a start. For a fraction of a second, life was normal as she reached her hand over the edge of the bed to touch Erik – and then the memory flooded back at the realization he was gone. Tears came again, shattering the peaceful hours of sleep.

"How will I get through this?" Andrea half mumbled.

She got out of the bed and mechanically showered. As she was dressing, she heard Arthur calling to her.

"Andrea, come here! Look at poor Sasha!" Arthur called out.

Arthur's tone was serious and Andrea moved quickly toward the sound of his voice. She found him in the foyer gazing up the staircase. Andrea followed his eyes upward, and there was Sasha, sitting on one of the upper stairs facing a blank wall.

A few minutes earlier, Arthur had noticed that Sasha had disappeared from her usual spot beside him at the kitchen table. It was uncharacteristic of her to leave his side with food on the table, so he was puzzled. He searched the backyard and all through the house and finally found her sitting on the staircase, staring at the wall.

"Come, sweet girl. Come be with us," Arthur spoke softly to Sasha but she didn't budge. It was as if she were glued to the spot on the stairs.

Then he pleaded, "Come Sasha. Come and let me hug you." She didn't even move her head. "What could be wrong with her?" he wondered.

Sasha wouldn't turn to face Andrea either. She didn't move from her position on the stairs. They both sensed she was angry with them and didn't want to make eye contact.

Sasha was grieving too and was very confused by what had happened over the past day.

"What do we do for Sasha, Andrea? She can't just sit and stare. I feel so bad for her." Arthur appealed to Andrea.

Andrea turned her palms up in the air while shaking her head in response, indicating she didn't know what to do either. Then she remembered that it had been Sasha's habit to go to the stairs when she had been admonished for something, or when she was angry because Erik had stolen one of her toys.

Andrea spoke. "Arthur, I think this may be her way of grieving. She's not letting us pet her and she's not giving any affection back to us. Her refusal of our love and comfort seems odd, but we can't know what she's experiencing. She loved Erik, too."

Arthur responded to Andrea's comment with a loving look of concern toward his dog.

No amount of coaxing would convince Sasha to move from her stationary location on the stairs. Andrea settled in next to her and was soon lost in thought. As was happening often these days, a familiar refrain began playing in her head, the classic Eagles ballad "Desperado."

As a teen, Andrea had worn out an 8-track cartridge playing the song again and again. She didn't literally envision herself as a lawless cowboy; rather, the song conjured for her the image of a lone wolf that needed no one. That lone wolf image was a core part of her being, a sense of self she would not fully shed until many years later.

While Andrea daydreamed the music in her head, Sasha just sat and stared until the doorbell rang.

The doorbell's ring and what followed saved Sunday morning. "Saved by the bell," as the proverb goes. Sasha leaped to her feet to greet the stranger.

It wasn't a stranger at all but rather their friend, Art. He was carrying a large dish of fragrant lasagna. He noticed Andrea's and Arthur's surprised looks and responded by saying, "When a family member dies, friends bring food!"

Art had summed up the situation in one sentence. The Chilcotes, including Sasha, had lost a member of their family. The family of three were inconsolable, but Art's gesture was welcomed.

The friends sat and talked for over an hour and for that brief time, Andrea felt comforted. Art scratched Sasha's ears and neck and she thanked him by curling up on the sofa next to him.

•

White Wolf and the Princess were watching and listening intently. "Princess, this is a critical day for Andrea."

"Why, White Wolf?" Princess asked.

White Wolf replied, "Because, on this day Andrea has an opportunity to express her feelings to her friends and be open to their care and concern for her.

You see, Andrea's always been the caretaker. She's very good at helping others when they are in pain, but she doesn't want to bother them with her needs. Do you understand that Princess?"

"I think so," the Princess replied.

"When I was Arthur's dog, I didn't always let him know when I was hurt. One time I stepped into a sticker bush and a got a thorn embedded in my pad. It hurt a lot but I didn't want our walk to end and I certainly didn't want to worry Arthur, so I just pretended I was fine. We walked for two hours on a desert path. That was the wrong decision though, because my foot got infected and the vet had to remove the thorn. It was so bad that I had to take medicine and stay inside for a week. If I had admitted that my foot was hurting, Arthur might have been able to fix it before it festered and caused a lot more pain."

"Is that what Andrea does, White Wolf, conceal her pain until it gets so bad she can't hide it any longer?" the Princess asked.

"That's exactly what she does. You're very perceptive, Princess," White Wolf added.

"This time, though, she just might experience a miracle – and we get to witness it." The twinkle returned to White Wolf's eye and it made the Princess smile.

•

Sunday morning flew by. Shortly after Art left, the doorbell rang again. It was a delivery of yellow roses from Andrea's friend, Tanya. The card said: "I'm sorry for the loss of your best friend, Erik."

Andrea thought to herself: "Hmmm . . . she too understands a dog can be a best friend."

Immediately, Andrea called Tanya to thank her and found voice messages waiting from others who had heard the news. She returned three calls. It seemed to be getting easier to talk rather than to be alone with her feelings.

Soon enough though, the house was empty of guests and the phone was silent. Andrea slipped back into her melancholy.

Andrea made her way upstairs to her office to work on the project she had begun the day before, selecting old photographs of Erik. Andrea had decided to make a poster with pictures of Erik to commemorate all the things they had done together. She tried to concentrate on her task, but the activity felt flat and dull.

As much as she tried to occupy her thoughts, it was impossible. The only thought, the only feeling she had, was profound sadness. It was as if neither the past nor the future existed – there was only the present . . . and the awful pain. Without knowing it or understanding it, Andrea was in full acceptance of the grief. It was all-consuming.

•

"White Wolf?"

"Yes Princess?"

"I think Andrea needs that miracle now." The Princess sounded very concerned. "Listen."

CHAPTER TWENTY-SIX

"Arthur, if this is all there is to life, I don't want to live. That's how I feel. If animals and people and love and joy can come into our lives and then leave us this empty, there must be no purpose to life."

Andrea had left her project, walked down the stairs and in a teary outburst, proclaimed to Arthur that she didn't want to live now that Erik had died.

"Arthur, I've always believed in a loving God that is the source of all the love there is. I believed the love Erik and I shared was an expression of that love. But if I could feel it one minute, then lose it so completely the next, maybe it wasn't real after all. Maybe none of it is real, and this life is just what we see, and then we die. Maybe we are nothing but bones and blood."

Arthur was frightened by Andrea's comments.

He tried to console her but he didn't know what to do or say. He hoped this strange madness would pass.

·

"Princess, I can see why you're concerned. Humans sometimes have odd ways of expressing themselves. It's very common for people to feel like they don't want to live, or to temporarily reject their faith when something painful or tragic occurs. Andrea's experiencing that now. It's what will make the miracle we are sending her even more significant. You'll see."

White Wolf gently stroked the Princess' fur and she relaxed. She trusted White Wolf.

REFLECTIONS
Receiving Compassion

After Erik's passing, Andrea was in a state of angry despair. Though it felt overwhelming at the time, the emotion was productive. She had experienced great losses before and yet had never experienced this normal stage of grief. Hers was amplified by the layers of loss stored away for years. She was purging emotion like the waves of the sea. Calcified remnants once alive were emerging. Little did she know they were lightening the load.

Arthur, who also was suffering Erik's loss, was doubly pained to hear Andrea express such futility. She was essentially saying she had nothing to live for when, in fact, as her husband and partner, he could clearly see all she had in her life. He had the graciousness to simply listen to her, rather than remind her of the life beyond Erik that existed. He somehow knew she must endure this dark night of the soul. Years later when asked what his greatest fear was that day, he replied: "My fear was that Andrea would go into her shell and not come out."

As White Wolf pointed out to the Princess, there is a big difference between not wanting to live – a feeling of hopelessness – and actually intending and planning to die. Andrea was experiencing the former amidst intense grief. On some level, she knew she was not going to get through this alone. A life-altering choice point was upon her. She finally asked herself, "Do I shrivel up in a corner or let someone love me through it?"

The choice she made seemed like the only choice. The only way she was going to endure the pain was with the support of other people. Even so, it was awkward and uncomfortable for her to need others in that way.

There is no scale or measuring system that weighs and compares loss. The loss may be human or animal, and result from death, divorce, or another form of separation. It may involve the loss of a limb, a job, or a lifestyle. Whatever the form, one way through is acceptance of the compassion of other human beings. Compassion does not judge the loss. It is simply a genuine expression of empathy for the suffering of another. The capacity for giving and receiving compassion is the essence of being a human.

Andrea demonstrated compassion for others.

The purposefulness she felt toward the work she did exemplified this quality. But the scales were unbalanced. Giving without receiving produces an empty bucket and an empty bucket is void of the tools of creation.

CHAPTER TWENTY-SEVEN

Monday morning came. Andrea was scheduled to lead a workshop and was committed to giving the participants the best of her work despite her personal situation. She became present and concentrated on the task at hand.

A funny thing happened that day. As Andrea fully and completely put her own concerns aside and listened to the very real and challenging problems these workshop participants faced in their own lives and work, she gained a new sense of perspective she hadn't been aware of before. She could simultaneously watch and listen to their stories, and even consider her own – yet experience it all at a slight but critical distance away from her raw pain.

When the group took breaks throughout the

day, as they did frequently, all of the emotion of the weekend rushed back and consumed her. When the session reconvened, Andrea was composed and effective. "Maybe," she thought, "there's light at the end of this dark tunnel. But who is this person I've become that can simultaneously feel awful grief and objectively observe myself having these new and strange feelings? Maybe I'm going crazy."

•

White Wolf was usually a very patient being. But even he wanted to rush in and explain it all to Andrea. He wanted to tell her that she was far from crazy – that, in fact, she was discovering a sacred secret. White Wolf knew that the "observer" Andrea called upon that day was the part of her that is part of All That Is. White Wolf also understood that Andrea had to learn these important lessons through experience, and no amount of explanation would substitute. He longed for the day when they could talk about it together.

•

The class ended at 3:00 p.m. and Andrea couldn't wait to get out of the windowless building and into her car. She was exhausted from the intensity of managing the day. Thankfully, her car was parked at the far end of the parking lot so no one saw her as she released her tears.

Andrea drove lost in thought. Habit guided her route and she was almost startled to find herself close to home, heading north on I–85 toward Lawrenceville. A vaguely frightening thought crossed her mind. "How did I get here – who has been driving the car?" she wondered aloud. Then, she noticed the new road construction ahead. Before her conscious mind could process the maze of lane shifts, she found herself gripping the wheel with both hands, battling for position with an aggressive driver on her right whose lane had merged with hers, while both of them narrowly missed a vehicle entering from the left shoulder.

It could not have been more than a few seconds of NASCAR-style driving, intense navigation at 70 mph, but once over, the emotional release set in. Safe now, Andrea exited the freeway and began to sob – the kind of sobbing that envelops the whole body in convulsions. Blinded by her tears, she pulled to the side of the road, stopped the car and put her face in her hands.

As Andrea's senses began to slowly return to

normal, she heard the music playing on the radio. Sarah McLachlan's "Angel" was dreamlike. "Is there an angel watching over me, or am I indeed losing my mind?" Andrea asked herself. She did not know the answer.

•

"White Wolf, that was scary," the Princess stated in a disapproving tone.

"Remember your concern yesterday Princess?" White Wolf asked. "Now she's beginning to get the message."

•

Andrea made her way back onto the road, numb. Entering the garage at home, she realized she couldn't bear going into the house. She knew the emptiness she would find there and longed for the protection of the classroom she had left.

She sat in the car inside the garage for so long Arthur came out to see what was keeping her. He found her head down, hands gripping the steering wheel, sobbing uncontrollably once again. The scene summed up the situation pretty quickly for

Arthur, even though he did not know of the freeway incident.

He tapped on the window. Andrea looked up, lowered the glass, but didn't get out of the car. "Come inside honey, you'll feel better soon."

"No, I can't go in. He's not there."

"You have to come in," Arthur pleaded. "This is our home."

"Arthur, just please give me a few more minutes. I'll be in soon." She knew she didn't want to be alone, and the house itself symbolized how alone she was without Erik.

Arthur didn't know what to do to make her get out of the car. He leaned into the open window and took her hands into his and said, "I know Erik is with us. I just know he is. Let's go inside and have a nice dinner. I heated Art's lasagna and made a salad. We'll go to bed early – maybe Erik will come to you in your dreams tonight."

Andrea gave in and opened the door. Robotically, she followed Arthur inside, the refrain of "Angel" still playing in her head.

CHAPTER TWENTY-EIGHT

Arthur noticed that Andrea seemed to sleep better that night than she had on the previous nights since Erik's passing.

When she came downstairs to breakfast, Arthur was already in the kitchen, reading the paper. Andrea moved slowly and deliberately, as if she was still half asleep. She walked to the hutch cabinet, opened it and took out a cup. She left the cabinet door open as she moved to the coffee pot and slowly poured the hot liquid. Arthur followed behind her, curious, and shut the cabinet door.

Next, she dreamily removed the coffee cream from the refrigerator, again forgetting to close the door. Arthur took care of it. They both sat down at the table and without any preamble, Andrea began to recount her dream from the night.

"I was walking along the bank of a wide river. It smelled like the ocean at low tide, and while I could see the larger waves in the distance, it was definitely just a tributary, a waterway that opens to the Pacific. In fact, it reminded me of the place we visited in Oregon where we watched eagles fish for silver salmon in the river. You remember that, right?"

"Yes, I do." Arthur replied, trying to be patient but anxious to hear the story.

Andrea continued, slowly and thoughtfully. "Anyway, I was just walking along the bank, barefoot. The sand was brown and cold on my feet. I felt that awful emptiness that has been coming and going since Saturday afternoon: a universe without Erik in it."

"The whole scene was painted in shades of brown and gray like my mood. I don't know how I remember the sepia colors and the pungent smells so vividly. The dream was very real; it's like it just happened. Like I just this minute returned from that place."

"All of a sudden I noticed a wisp of light across the river. It rose from the edge of the surf made by the waves lapping the shore. I kept walking, thinking I imagined the wisp. But it grew into a starburst of light and then a form appeared – the form of a giant white animal – wolf-like in shape, though much bigger than an actual wolf. The form wasn't solid. It was made of light, and while this all sounds a bit frightening now, I wasn't afraid. This Being, this white wolfish Being, exuded awesome love, and I called it to me with my mind. It spoke to me."

Totally intrigued, Arthur asked, "What did it say?"

"Well, I'll get to that. At first glance I thought it was Erik . . . his soul perhaps. But when I reached out to touch it, I couldn't feel Erik at all. I knew it wasn't Erik, despite its loving kindness. I began to cry. Fell to my knees sobbing, actually. When I woke up the pillowcase was still soaking wet with tears. "

"'Andrea,' the Being said, 'you look very sad.'"

"'I am sad,' I said. 'I lost my precious dog, my best friend, Erik.'"

"'I know,' the Being said, and touched my shoulder."

"'You know? Who are you?' I asked. I don't know how to explain it, but I felt completely safe and loved. I trusted him."

"'I am White Wolf, Erik's guardian angel and teacher,' he replied. 'I am with him now.'"

"Arthur, I know this all sounds crazy. But I believed – and still believe – everything he said to me!"

"Go on," Arthur said patiently, anxious to hear

the rest of the dream.

"So I began to speak, and asked the Being questions. For some reason I got very agitated. I said, 'White Wolf, I have begun to doubt that Erik's spirit lives on because I can't sense his love. I think he might really be gone. Oh, I know his body is gone. But I always thought I would be able to sense Erik's love, even after he died. I always believed that we – animals and people – have a spirit, a soul that survives death. But I can't connect with Erik, no matter how hard I try. Surely if the love I have for him is real, I should be able to feel it now. Maybe we are just bones and blood, and life on earth is all there is.'"

"'Oh, Andrea, my dear,' White Wolf began, 'your love for Erik and his for you are real, and his spirit did survive his death. He is here with me, but you can't feel him because now you must grieve.'"

"'Why?' I asked. 'Why must it be so painful and so empty? Why can't I have even a glimpse that he is whole and well?'"

"'Andrea, Erik is your special teacher. You know that. Of the many gifts and lessons he gave you during his life, none compare to the most important one of all – the one you are experiencing now. His greatest teaching is that love never dies. You will sense Erik's spirit soon, but not until you grieve the loss of his form. And Erik will come back to you.'"

"Arthur, now I was confused. Excited, heart racing, but still confused. I didn't understand and told White Wolf, 'I don't get it – why do I have to suffer? Why do I need to go through this?'"

"He replied, 'Because it is part of being a human, Andrea. There is a circle of life on earth – love, loss and eventually, redemption from the bitter pain. You have had other painful losses in your life and you didn't always take the time to experience them in the moment. When you block out pain or try to think it away, you actually store it up. It never goes away. If Erik came to you now, you might miss out on this important lesson. You must experience and move through the grief instead of avoiding it.'"

"'I'm still not sure I understand,' I said. 'But then I remembered something else he had said and asked him, 'You said Erik would come back to me. Did you mean' . . . I hesitated . . . 'did you mean like this, in a dream, or . . . ?'"

"White Wolf interrupted my questions. 'Andrea, Erik will come back to you as a new puppy. But don't look for him now – your job is to grieve. I'll return with the details when it is time.'"

"And then just before he disappeared, he said, almost as if he were cautioning me, 'You must remain aware of something important, Andrea. Erik went out as an eagle, and will come back as a butterfly.'"

"Then I woke up." She hesitated, and a puzzled look crossed her face.

"I just remembered something else. The music – I heard familiar music. Were you playing my Grateful Dead CD, Arthur?"

Arthur laughed. "Not a chance."

"Hmmm, that's odd," Andrea murmured. "I must have dreamed that too."

Arthur and Andrea sat quietly for a long moment. Arthur had been staring out the kitchen window contemplating everything Andrea had said about her dream. He turned toward Andrea, looked into her eyes and spoke.

"You must be patient. Follow White Wolf's advice. I believe that Erik will return to you, to us. We'll find him together."

REFLECTIONS
Transformation

Who we are is a product of the interaction of our higher purpose with our choices and history. Who our parents were, and the genes they contributed in a seemingly but far from random process, produce the modeling clay. We make choices, conscious or unconscious, in response to the experiences we are dealt and in response to the whisper of a greater spiritual purpose.

At the time of Erik's death, Andrea had been building her business for seven years. Her work was and felt purposeful. Her sense was that she was here on earth to help people grow and change in transformational ways, and she was doing that by developing their ability to define and achieve important goals. She cared about the people she coached and trained. Little did she realize the gratitude they felt for the impact her work made.

Transformational work in the world requires one to walk a path of transformation. One cannot know another without knowing oneself. Erik's death helped Andrea see what she had been blind to before.

Any life contains suffering. By remaining present to the suffering, versus avoiding or burying it, we come to know its role and purpose in defining who we are. Paradoxically, we transcend pain by experiencing it fully. As hard as it was for Andrea to understand the message, "Just grieve," it was perhaps the most important gift of counsel she had ever received.

"When we deal with our suffering truthfully and completely, it is not that the pain is less real, but there is indeed a lesson to be learned and, even more, purpose and direction to be gained from it. Our whole trajectory can be changed through suffering. Our truth, which is often disguised or hidden by the layers of ego we use as a shield against hardship, starts to break through. We begin to fall apart, and in the process, we find the unique nature and purpose of our existence, and our reason for being put here on this earth. It is when we find this inner core that we start to transcend the pain and begin the journey down the road intended for us."

Matthew Gewirtz

The Gift of Grief:
Finding Peace, Transformation and Renewed Life
after Great Sorrow

CHAPTER TWENTY-NINE

Over the next few days Andrea's spirits begin to improve with the promise that Erik would return. Arthur was glad to see Andrea improving but he was not putting too much faith in Andrea's dream of White Wolf.

One Saturday morning at breakfast, Andrea had a worried look on her face. Arthur asked, "Is something wrong, Andrea? You look troubled."

Even though Andrea's sharp pain seemed to be easing, Arthur deeply understood the state she was in. He remembered his own feelings when he lost the Princess. He recalled how much he had grieved for her and he had pure empathy for what Andrea was experiencing after losing her best friend.

Andrea responded to Arthur's question with her

own question, "White Wolf hasn't come back to me again since the first dream. Why hasn't he given me some sign that Erik is coming back?"

Arthur took a deep breath knowing that what he was about to say could create an upheaval in what was shaping up as a peaceful weekend. "Andrea, Erik was a wonderful dog. We both loved him, but you shouldn't put all your hopes in your dream. I really hope he comes back, too, but I'm concerned that you're putting too much credit in your dream."

Andrea responded with a curious look. Her sagging shoulders and drooping head rose swiftly as a look of determination came over her face.

"I believe White Wolf's message, Arthur. I just think I'm being tested and I don't understand the purpose. Why doesn't he come back and tell me more? I want to know when I'm going to be finished grieving. When am I going to be done with this?"

Arthur didn't have an answer, but White Wolf did.

•

White Wolf spoke to the gentle spirit beside him. "Erik, she's still not ready."

"How do you know, White Wolf?" Erik asked.

"Well, Erik, I'll try to explain, though it might be hard for you to understand."

"You see, human grief isn't something that gets turned on and off. I'm afraid that Andrea interpreted my message to her as if there was an on/off switch and that one day soon, the feeling would end."

"The way it really works is this. Days go by and very slowly, the feelings of separation and aloneness get filled by care and compassion, productivity, and eventually – even joy. It happens gradually, often as a result of allowing others to show kindness, and returning those kindnesses through helping others. Andrea will feel your unconditional love again when she offers her own love without reservation and fear. And she will, I know it."

Erik thanked White Wolf, even though he really didn't fully understand. Later, he recounted White Wolf's explanation to his friend the Princess.

"Erik, you're so silly," the Princess responded. "You should understand this better than anyone. When I died and left Arthur, you helped fill that empty place in his heart while he was grieving. Remember how you cared for him? Oh, he thought he was caring for you, rushing home from work to give you treats and take you on beach walks. But you were helping him too, keeping his heart open even while he hurt for me."

"I think I get it, Princess," Erik said. "When sad or tragic things happen, people have choices. They can stay mired in their sadness and become hardened or resentful. Or they can pretend nothing happened, like Andrea used to do. But if they just stay open and hopeful, people (and dogs!) will show up to help."

"That's exactly right, Erik. Dogs especially!"

They both laughed.

CHAPTER THIRTY

Over the next weeks, the family worked hard at maintaining some semblance of normal activity, but Andrea was feeling anything but normal. She relished long talks with friends who understood how important Erik was in her life and she was grateful that she had chosen to open up and confide in them. She still desperately longed to stroke Erik's fur and look into his eyes, and, at the same time, she felt very much loved by the people around her.

Unfortunately, she was not feeling love from the canine who shared their home. Sasha continued to be standoffish to Andrea and to Arthur as well. She moped around the house. Andrea was very much aware that Sasha was not responding to her attempts at companionship, and she was torn between her compassion for Sasha and her resentment that Sasha seemed to be withholding affection at a time Andrea needed it most.

"Arthur, we've got to do something for Sasha," Andrea stated. "Maybe she needs another dog for friendship. I know I could sure use the love of another adult dog."

"Andrea, if you really believe that Erik is going to come back, just wait. Sasha will be fine."

"It's true that I'm concerned about Sasha's well being, and I'm also concerned about my own. White Wolf didn't say 'when' Erik would return, just that he would. It could be months!" Andrea was becoming intent on an idea and wanted Arthur's agreement. She had a plan.

She went on, "With so many dogs in the world needing to be rescued and cared for, I know there has to be one who needs us and will love us back."

Arthur threw up his hands. He knew it was pointless to argue with her.

That afternoon, Andrea decided to call the man who had found Sasha for them. She so craved to have a big fluffy animal back in her life and maybe Joseph would know of a good Samoyed dog to rescue.

Andrea contacted Joseph and told him the story of Erik's death and that she was looking for an older male Samoyed. Joseph responded by saying, "Andrea, guess what? I have Sasha's father back. Trump is nine years old now and needs a home. He's spent many years as a champion show dog, and deserves a family now who will love and care for him."

Andrea felt a well of elation. Trump! She had met Trump years before. He was a gentle, loving creature and he and Sasha had been close companions. Andrea covered the phone's mouthpiece with her hand and excitedly exclaimed to Arthur, "Joseph has Trump! We can have him – he's nine years old and needs a home!"

Arthur began to protest, saying that Trump was too old. Then, mid-sentence he looked at Andrea's face and changed his position. Without another thought, Arthur said, "okay, but Joseph's not putting him on a plane. We'll drive to Minnesota to get him."

And so they did.

•

Andrea and Arthur drove through the night and well into the next day with Sasha in the back seat. When they got to Joseph's house, they found Trump in terrible condition. His fur was matted and his teeth were in bad shape. It was obvious that the dog had been neglected for some time. As they approached him, Trump shook with fear of what might happen to him.

Sadly, Trump had been a champion show dog and lived that life until his usefulness was gone. John explained, "Once these show dogs are past their prime, sometimes the owners just ignore them, or throw them away when they are too old to perform any more. He was a beautiful show dog once and I know with grooming and proper care he can be beautiful again. It'll just take some work."

Andrea and Arthur gently introduced themselves to Trump. He must have known they would love him and care for him. He moved toward them and gave the universal signal, the canine tail wag.

Trump was then reintroduced to Sasha, his daughter whom he had not seen since her adoption several years before. Amazingly, the dogs seemed to recognize each other. It was literally a family reunion and both looked as if they had been waiting for this moment for years. Sasha showed more spirit than she had in many weeks and soon the two were huddled together in the car for the long trip home.

When the family arrived back in Atlanta, the dogs were released in the backyard for an opportunity to run and spend pent-up energy from the long ride.

Sasha looked so happy to have a companion and seemed content once again.

Trump followed Sasha back through the doggy door and into the family room. He took one look around the room and spotted the coffee table. Then something very odd happened. He walked over to the coffee table, jumped up on it, and stood. It was as if he had taken a long journey and now it was time to "show."

Trump maintained his show dog pose until Andrea went over and hugged him. She whispered to him, "Oh Trump, from now on you get to be a special Chilcote dog. You don't have to perform any longer. All you have to do now is allow yourself to be loved." She nuzzled his neck and spoke softly to him until it felt to her that he understood.

•

As it turned out, Trump was barely housebroken and had few manners. He pooped and peed in the house for several days until he learned that he would be taken out whenever he needed to go. Sasha continued to enjoy Trump's companionship, but Andrea had her hands full.

Trump seemed to love the safety of his crate and

had slept there since arriving at the Chilcote home. Andrea made sure the door was always open so that he had the freedom to come and go at will. She never wanted him to think that he'd be confined again.

In the short time he had been with them, Trump had proven to have a strange habit of taking things. Oddly, items of all types would go missing in the house. Andrea and Arthur were quickly learning to look in Trump's crate when anything was missing. One day, shortly after Trump's arrival, Andrea had gathered up the blankets in his crate to freshen them. Out tumbled a full roll of toilet paper, one of Arthur's slippers, the missing leather glove a house guest had left and a Mr. Sketch scented marker. Each day seemed to bring a new surprise.

On Friday of Trump's first week in his new home, Andrea placed a package of frozen chicken breasts to thaw on the kitchen counter. She was nonchalant about the simple task and returned to her upstairs office. Little did she realize that Trump, a much larger dog than Erik or Sasha, could surf the counters with ease.

The minute she disappeared, Trump walked over to the counter and stole the package. He ate the whole thing with the zeal of one who thought he was never going to be fed again. Then he disappeared into his crate, carrying the Styrofoam chicken package with him.

With a funny feeling gnawing at her, Andrea returned to the kitchen for a glass of water. Noticing bits of plastic wrap strewn across the floor, she looked for the chicken package on the counter. Seeing that it was missing, she followed the bits of debris all the way to Trump's crate.

Not surprisingly, Trump was present, nonchalantly cleaning bits of chicken paper off his furry paws. The white Styrofoam tray was tucked under a blue blanket, as if it were a treasure wrapped for later use.

Andrea didn't know whether to laugh or scold the dog. She yelled out to Arthur, "Come quickly, Arthur. Look at what Trump has done! He's eaten our dinner – the whole package of raw chicken!"

Standing in front of the crate with his hands on his hips, Arthur asked Andrea, "Were we crazy for bringing another dog into this house?"

Andrea considered Arthur's question carefully. She really hoped they hadn't taken on another unruly rescue, because she had already convinced herself they were destined to raise a new puppy soon. But that worry was immediately replaced by another: concern for Trump's health.

"Arthur, we're committed to him now. And I'd

better call Dr. Pat to see what we should do about this chicken before he becomes ill. He ate two whole pounds!"

Arthur opened his mouth to tell Andrea that Trump would be fine – and then he paused. He realized that Andrea had just what she needed right now – someone to care for and fret over. He smiled as she called their beloved veterinarian, and imagined that Dr. Pat smiled too.

•

The decision to bring Trump into the family continued to be good for Sasha. The bond between the two dogs seemed to grow stronger each day. Trump and Sasha were inseparable. They even walked in sync with one another, much like whales do swimming in pods in the ocean. A house guest commented one evening, "Look at the two of them. Their movements are tandem-like. How can they do that? They look like those beautiful white Lipizzaner stallions!"

It was a joy to watch Trump relish life. He was nine years old, and it was as if he had never been allowed to be a puppy. He would take Sasha's toys, and hide them inside his crate. She didn't mind at all.

Andrea watched happily. She, too, was growing

to love Trump. And, as goofy as his antics were, she enjoyed caring for him. Even more, she felt gratified by the fact that she and Arthur had given this sweet older dog a happy life. Still, she missed Erik and often thought of White Wolf's words: "Erik will come back to you as a new puppy . . . I'll return with the details when it is time."

"White Wolf, where are you?" Andrea mused in her melancholy.

REFLECTIONS
Surrender

The dark night of the soul is not a night. It is a passageway through time. It is a period of profound aloneness that precedes transformation.

Andrea was not literally alone. But the being for and from whom she felt complete unconditional love, Erik, was gone. Her dark night began when he passed and, while she was functioning externally in the world, the light was out inside.

There was a death occurring beyond Erik's literal death. The old aspects of Andrea's personality that no longer served her were dying. These opportunities present themselves to us in a myriad of ways. Often the ego blocks change and we rationalize it away. Death provides a forced surrender, and surrender is required for transformation.

Nothing satisfied Andrea during this period of time, as nothing external ever does. Trump provided distraction, friends provided an outlet for emotional release and Arthur provided a loving anchor – a grounding in possibility for future joy. All of these were useful but not sufficient. What was missing for Andrea was a conduit to the Divine. Erik had served as her connection to Source itself. Now, nothing outside of her could replace this. She would have to find it within.

"You say I am repeating
Something I have said before. I shall say it again.
Shall I say it again? In order to arrive there,
To arrive where you are, to get from where you are not,
You must go by a way wherein there is no ecstasy."

T.S. Eliot

"East Coker" The Four Quartets

CHAPTER THIRTY-ONE

The weeks passed.

Andrea and Arthur had been invited back to their beloved Arizona for a wedding. It was the wedding of a special friend, the woman who had taught the workshop years prior that had helped Andrea decide to start her own business. Linda had been instrumental in helping Andrea start her business and Andrea wanted to celebrate the special day with her.

Prior to Erik's death, Linda's original invitation had been extended to include him. She considered Erik part of the Chilcote family and a friend as well. Her outdoor wedding in Prescott, Arizona could easily accommodate canine guests.

Now, Andrea didn't think she could bear the trip knowing Erik was supposed to be with them. Arthur persuaded her that the trip would do her good, and it would be great to see Linda and be back in Arizona again.

Andrea and Arthur hired a baby sitter to stay with Sasha and Trump, and determined they would have a wonderful time in Arizona.

•

The wedding was lovely and the weather perfect. Afterward, Andrea and Arthur left the Prescott area to vacation in nearby Sedona. The luxurious resort where Andrea and Arthur stayed had biking and hiking trails leading directly from the hotel.

Andrea awakened very early the morning after the wedding, and felt more energy than she had known in many weeks. She decided to go for a pre-dawn bike ride. By the time she got back, the first light was appearing over the mountains. She hurried back to the room and tugged at Arthur to go for a hike with her.

"No way!" was Arthur's response, and he turned back over in the bed and covered his head. He was on vacation and was enjoying sleeping in.

"Well, I guess I'm on my own. That's okay too!" she thought.

Andrea pulled on her hiking boots and grabbed the car keys. As she drove, she thought about the trails available for hiking. It was an easy decision with the sun coming up over Bell Rock Trail. It would be beautiful.

She parked the car amidst the wonderland of red rocks pressing themselves against a backdrop of azure blue forming in the morning sky. Deep green juniper bushes helped mark the trailhead. Andrea was acutely aware of everything as the colors jumped out at her. The three-dimensional effects of the rocks were movie-like, as if she had on 3-D glasses.

She started up the trail and felt more alive and more settled than she had felt since Erik's death.

Andrea hiked upward and around the huge rock, stirring the red dust as she moved along. Then, something tugged at her consciousness. It was so light and gentle, it could have been a wisp of a cloud moving across her mind . . . but it wasn't.

•

"Erik . . . Erik!" White Wolf called out.

"You have been resting as I advised. It's now time to prepare for your journey. First though, we have planned something very special for you. Come, take a look. Tell me what you see."

"It's beautiful! There's a path, White Wolf, that is the most amazing place I've ever seen. The mountains seem to glow with a rusty red color, and the path itself is made of the same red soil that shimmers in the sunlight. The trees are dark green; I can smell them too. Umm . . . musty and earth-like. I miss the earth, White Wolf."

"Those are juniper trees, Erik. I thought you'd like them. And the rocks are part of a beautiful area in Arizona called Sedona. That's the Bell Rock Pathway."

"But Erik, that's not all of the surprise. Look more closely – way up the trail."

"It's Andrea!"

"Yes, Erik." White Wolf replied with a huge smile.

"She's alone . . . walking slowly as if she's enjoying the scenery too. She seems more peaceful today. Is she feeling better, White Wolf?" Erik asked.

"Why don't you find out Erik? You can join her on the path and sense it for yourself. It's time."

"Now – right now? What should I do, White Wolf? Will she be able to see me? I'm not a dog anymore; how will she know it's me?"

"Andrea will know it's you," White Wolf answered.

"She won't see you, but she will sense your spirit and love. She might make pictures in her mind and imagine you're a dog walking beside her. That's okay, that's how humans do it. Go ahead now, it's time."

So right then and there, Erik gathered all the love of All That Is and walked next to his beloved Andrea on the Bell Rock Pathway.

•

A knowing smile brightened Andrea's face. "Could it be?" she thought, as tears formed.

She walked more slowly up the trail now, afraid that any sudden movement would cause the magic to vanish. Yet it only strengthened as she walked. Andrea felt Erik's peaceful presence surrounding her. It was so real that she wanted to reach down and pet him.

Andrea was filled with awe. Tears fell freely, but this time they were almost happy tears. And, for the first time since Erik's death, Andrea had the assurance that what White Wolf had told her was true.

It was time.

CHAPTER THIRTY-TWO

Andrea was still drinking in the sights and sounds around her as she made the short drive back to the hotel. Once again, the music on the radio seemed to speak to her as if divinely arranged. George Harrison spoke directly into her heart as he sang of hope, the kind of hope one gets through pure soul connection in the midst of despair. She paused in the parking lot of the resort, lost in the moment until the song was complete. Then, with a shiver, shook off the feeling, burst out of the car and raced for the room.

"Arthur, wake up! It's nearly seven o'clock!"

"Seven o'clock?" the groggy Arthur grouched. "So what? We're on vacation!"

"Oh, don't waste the day!" Andrea responded excitedly. "It's a marvelous day. I can't wait to tell you what happened."

Arthur got up, showered, and soon joined Andrea on the patio of their casita. The sun was still low in the sky and cast a yellow glow on the mountains as it does so uniquely in late August in Arizona.

"So what exciting thing happened before normal people are even out of bed?" Arthur asked.

"Erik came to me," Andrea began, "right over there on the trail."

She continued. "I couldn't sleep. I woke up at three a.m. and dozed a bit, woke again at four, then went for a bike ride to burn off some energy. Isn't that the craziest thing?"

"Anyway, about four-thirty I came back to see if you wanted to hike. Don't you remember me waking you?"

"Vaguely," Arthur thought to himself, but nodded.

Andrea continued. "I drove to Bell Rock. I felt compelled to go to the trailhead and walk. I was the only person out there. The light was eerie; the mountains seemed to glow as the sun rose."

"I was walking along, looking at the ground. I brushed against a juniper tree and looked up and saw that the path suddenly curved and narrowed. I stopped to take in the pungent scent and gorgeous view. As I turned away, I felt Erik next to me. As if I could reach down and touch him – he was really there!"

"Did you see him?" Arthur asked.

"Not with my eyes," Andrea replied. "I imagined that I saw him and that I could reach down and touch his fur. I felt him. I'm certain of that."

"Well, I believe you," Arthur said. "Now are you more certain that Erik's spirit is alive? Do you feel better now?"

"Yes – and curious. Do you remember my dream of White Wolf?"

"Of course," Arthur replied.

"Well, White Wolf said I would sense Erik's spirit again. And he also said that at that time, he, White Wolf, would come to me with details of Erik's return. So now I'm wondering if I'll sense or dream White Wolf again soon," Andrea said thoughtfully.

"Anything could happen." Arthur said with a happy twinkle in his eye.

•

The rest of the trip was uneventful.

Arthur thought that Andrea seemed herself again. Andrea enjoyed the remainder of the stay in Sedona and, at the same time, looked forward to getting home to get some rest. She hadn't been able to sleep in Sedona and when one does not sleep, one does not dream.

CHAPTER THIRTY-THREE

The man was watching Andrea from a distance. She was intent on her study and didn't notice him at first. Books about dream interpretation surrounded her on the floor.

The man, Erin Michael, decided to approach her when it appeared to him that she was disconcerted. He took pride in the selection of books his store offered and wanted to help if he could. He touched her on the shoulder.

"Can I help you, my dear?" Erin Michael gently asked.

"Oh . . . no, I don't think so . . . " Andrea stammered, then burst into tears. She looked into his kind blue eyes and sensed his compassion.

"Well, maybe so. You see I'm looking for my dog.

I mean, my dog, Erik, died and . . . " She choked on the words. "Oh. It's complicated and you'll think I'm silly, I suppose. But I've been having these dreams..."

"Dreams are never silly," Erin Michael said. "Tell me more about what you are looking for – I'll try to help you." He sat down on the floor beside her.

Before she knew it, Andrea had told Erin Michael the whole story, including the dream about White Wolf and her experience in Sedona. When she finished, she tried to search his eyes, but he appeared to be in a trance. He breathed slowly and deeply, then spoke.

"Andrea, I want you to contact my friend, Susan, at Morningstar Kennels. She lives in Mississippi, and she has a dog, a Siberian Husky, who just had puppies. You must follow my instructions. This has been set up so that there's no chance of a mistake."

"But . . . but how will I know it's him? What if I pick the wrong puppy?"

"You will know him by his voice and his eyes," Erin Michael replied.

•

Andrea awoke in a fog. Even though she was in her own bed in Georgia, she could faintly smell the salt air of the Oregon coast . . . the smell she recalled from the first White Wolf dream.

"White Wolf? White Wolf, are you there?!"

Arthur, awakened by the sound of Andrea's voice, looked at the clock beside the bed. Nine o'clock! He reached out to Andrea and hugged her fully awake.

"What is it?" Arthur asked. "Did White Wolf come into your dreams?"

"I don't know . . . " Andrea murmured softly.

Still groggy, Arthur sat up in bed. Even though he was half asleep, he saw the wonder in Andrea's face. He pulled himself up onto the pillow.

"Tell me what you remember honey."

Andrea told Arthur about her dream of being in the bookstore, and of the kind man, Erin Michael, who told her to contact Susan in Mississippi. When she got to that part, disappointment crossed her face as she realized this had been only a dream.

"Arthur, it was a dream! How will I find Susan?"

"Well Andrea," Arthur replied. "If White Wolf sent you that dream, you'll find her. Let's Google her. Now."

And so they did.

Andrea left out an important detail when she relayed the bookstore dream to Arthur. Erin Michael had told her to contact Susan at Morningstar Kennels in Mississippi. She forgot everything except Susan,

Mississippi and Siberian Husky. It was not a problem however, because the internet search produced Susan's website immediately. Morningstar Kennels in Florence, MS. Andrea looked at Arthur and could barely contain herself.

"Arthur, he said Susan's kennel was named Morningstar! I forgot that until this moment – it must be the one!"

Arthur was amazed. He could not believe what he was seeing and thought to himself, "There must be some logical explanation for this." As open minded as he was trying to be, this was weird!

"Andrea, let's not jump to conclusions. Let's see what else we find in Mississippi."

Andrea took a deep breath and slowly scanned the other search results. She searched Siberian Husky breeders to see if maybe there was another site she had overlooked. None, nada, this was the only one. Deep in her heart she just knew this was where Erik would choose to be born.

Then, for just a moment, she felt conflict. She recalled how many homeless dogs there are and thought of the precious Princess and Trump, two loving dogs that had desperately needed homes when they joined the Chilcote family. Then she remembered something Erin Michael had said to her in her dream,

"This has been set up so that there is no chance of a mistake."

"Arthur?"

"Yes, Andrea?"

"What am I going to say to Susan? 'A man came to me in a dream and said you were his friend, and that you have my new puppy sent from Erik in Heaven?'"

Arthur laughed out loud. "No, Andrea. Just tell her you found her online and that we want the pick of her next litter."

"Oh," Andrea smiled. "I guess it's that easy." She picked up the phone to call Susan and Arthur walked out of the room. As he walked away, the phone was already ringing. Andrea covered the mouthpiece.

"Arthur." Andrea called after him. When he turned back, she said, "I heard the music again. It was playing in the bookstore."

Arthur paused, looked at her curiously, and went on his way.

•

"White Wolf, you are very clever," said the Princess. She, White Wolf and Erik had been watching and listening.

"Yes," Erik added. "How did you come up with

this idea? It's perfect!"

"Well, Erik and Princess," White Wolf began, "it really doesn't have to be complicated. Love never dies – I've said this before and you both understand. But Andrea is still learning, and we have to make it rather foolproof for her. She is learning to trust her feelings and intuition, and I want to help reinforce that learning. Humans often dream of people and animals that have died. Many times they're really connecting with them – though they tell themselves it was just a dream. Andrea won't be able to say it was just a dream when she sees what happens next."

•

Susan Field-Boyd of Florence Morningstar Kennel answered the phone. She and Andrea had a cordial conversation. Andrea told Susan about losing Erik – that he had died and she had been very distraught, nothing else. Susan talked about her dogs and her philosophy. She highlighted the fact that she breeds for loving temperaments. "Sweetness and gentility" were the words she used. She said she socializes her puppies in her own home "showering them with love and kisses to develop their unconditionally loving personalities."

Andrea was comforted. While Siberian Huskies were gorgeous, Susan emphasized character traits over physical characteristics. Erik would be able to return to this world with the loving assistance of a caring midwife.

That same day Andrea mailed a check to Florence Morningstar Kennel to reserve the pick of the next litter, just as she and Arthur had agreed.

REFLECTIONS
Heaven On Earth

"What if you slept, and what if in your sleep
you dreamed, and what if in your dream you
went to heaven and there you picked a strange
and beautiful flower, and what if when you
awoke you had the flower in your hand?
Ah, what then?"

Samuel Taylor Coleridge

What then, indeed.

Did Andrea experience a miracle, or was her
"flower" evidence that the line between heaven and
earth is blurred, not the barrier one might believe it
to be?

"Here and gone." Our language is not sufficient to
express the complexity of life and death, our conscious
brains too mired in doubt, asking "how" instead of
marveling in gratitude.

This realization changed everything for Andrea.
What might it change for you?

CHAPTER THIRTY-FOUR

"I don't like water! What's this water all about?"

Erik sensed he was safe and in a loving environment. But he could barely move in the small, crowded, wet space. "And what are these tiny puppies doing in here with me?"

He was given no answers, but was allowed to remember two things at the moment of his birth: "She will find me, and I will be called Amigo."

CHAPTER THIRTY-FIVE

Time passed and a couple of weeks after their first conversation, Susan sent an email message to Andrea. It read:

Dear Andrea,

I received your check for a puppy from the litter that will be born in about a month. I know you requested one of those dogs and I am not trying to push a different dog on you – please know that. But I have a male Husky puppy that was born on October 7th.

I know this sounds strange, but this particular puppy makes me think of you all the time. I can't help myself and I think you should see this one. You and your husband should meet this dog.

He's pure white. I'll mail you some pictures if you would like; meanwhile, I posted a picture of his mother on my website. Her name is White Wolf.

Warm regards,

Susan

"White Wolf!?" Andrea re-read the note, then immediately searched Susan's website. There was beautiful White Wolf, the puppy's mother.

"Hmmm," she thought, "that's enough evidence for me. This must be the puppy!"

Andrea couldn't wait to tell Arthur about Susan's email. Unfortunately, he was not as easily convinced.

"I don't know, Andrea, this all just seems too strange to me," Arthur responded. Then, seeing the scowl on Andrea's face, he said, "Wait until the pictures arrive. Maybe I'll have a better feeling when I see them."

That Friday morning, Andrea watched from an upstairs window as the mail carrier filled their box. Once he was gone, Andrea forced herself to walk patiently to the box.

Opening the mailbox, she found an envelope addressed to her from Morningstar Kennels. At first she held her breath. Then she raced into the house, calling to Arthur while ripping open the envelope.

Standing just inside the front door, she pulled the pictures out. Andrea gasped as she glanced at the photograph on top, then felt nearly faint. The rest of the mail fell to the floor just as Arthur entered the foyer.

"What's the matter – are you okay?" Arthur asked, concerned.

Andrea held out a trembling hand. She held the picture out at arm's length, in front of the treasured portrait of Erik that Kerri had sketched years before. "Look," she said weakly.

The likeness was incredible. Even more astounding, she got the sense from his eyes that this very young pup was actually a wise, old animal. It mattered not that Erik had been a Samoyed; this tiny Husky was identical in so many ways. And those eyes . . .

Arthur raised a brow, took a deep breath and said quietly, "Call Susan and see if we can come meet the puppy. This weekend."

That very day Andrea and Arthur made plans to visit Mississippi.

•

On Saturday, the Chilcotes loaded Sasha and Trump into the car and set out on the six-hour drive to Florence, Mississippi to meet their new friend. While it would be another four weeks before he was weaned from his mother and they could bring him home, Andrea was joyful. She was convinced that this was the puppy. Arthur was still a bit skeptical but did nothing to dampen her resolve.

The day of the trip was a typical rainy day in the South. The drive from Atlanta to Mississippi was tricky, with steady rain alternating with mist and heavy fog. It was raining hard when they arrived at Susan's home.

As they pulled into the driveway, Arthur paused and looked worriedly at Andrea. "I'd like Susan to bring all the puppies out together," he said. "I don't want her to identify the one she has in mind for us."

Andrea tried to hide her smile as she looked into Arthur's eyes and earnestly said, "That's a good idea." When she looked up, Susan was walking toward the car through the pouring rain. Fortunately, she was empty-handed except for an umbrella.

Warm greetings were shared and Susan agreed when Andrea conveyed Arthur's request.

Susan led Andrea and Arthur into her kitchen, and invited Arthur to sit on the floor at the opposite side of the room. She exited and Andrea waited by the kitchen door, hardly able to contain her excitement.

Susan returned promptly with a laundry basket of wiggling puppies. It was quite a sight! As she passed Andrea, she pointed discreetly and whispered. "This is the one."

Andrea and Arthur observed as Susan removed the four-week-old puppies from the basket. They smiled at the furry little balls that were still so young they were weak-kneed and uncoordinated. They tended to congregate together and hover near Susan. That is, all but one.

One puppy, *the* puppy, immediately ran, albeit in a wobbly fashion, across the kitchen floor to Arthur and scampered onto his lap. It was as if he had to first convince his daddy of who he was. There was much licking and wiggling going on as Arthur caressed the puppy. After a couple of minutes, satisfied that he had done his job, the puppy made his way back across the floor and burrowed in behind Andrea's feet.

None of the other puppies had left Susan's side.

Andrea and Susan joined Arthur on the floor to play with the puppies. Just then, the room lightened as the sun came through the windows. All three were startled by the sudden change. It had been raining for three days and now, at this special moment, the earth found blue sky between the clouds. Arthur's eyes met Andrea's; she knew he recognized the miracle.

Susan exclaimed, "Let's take the puppies outside so you can observe them with their mother, White Wolf."

Arthur and Susan filled their arms with puppies, leaving Andrea with the special one. Following Susan outside, Arthur whispered to Andrea, "This puppy is Erik, Andrea. I was sure of it the moment the sun came out."

Andrea beamed. "I know," she said softly.

Just as the words left her, she tripped on the slippery porch and to her horror, dropped the puppy! He tumbled down the steps into Susan's backyard, thankfully taking the fall gracefully. Andrea shrieked at her mistake as she scooped him into her arms again. The puppy yelped, seeming to scold her. "Well, that sound is sure familiar," she thought.

Andrea suddenly remembered something Erin Michael had said to her in the dream. "You will know him by his voice and his eyes."

The eyes were an obvious match . . . but a puppy voice? Upon dropping him, Andrea got to hear his scream. It was identical to Erik's who had used it to express displeasure, an example being the approach of a needle at Dr. Pat's office.

Assured by Susan that the puppy was fine, Andrea carried him to White Wolf's pen, where the others had already begun to nurse. He readily joined them for his meal.

While the puppies were nursing, Andrea walked back to the car.

Sasha and Trump had been waiting patiently in the car for the rain to end, and they needed to stretch their legs. Andrea snapped on their leashes and let them out of the car. They were a safe distance from the puppies and separated by a chain link fence.

The special puppy spotted Sasha and Trump. He left his siblings and his mother's milk and ran in his puppy-like fashion to the fence. Andrea, Arthur, and Susan watched as he stretched and strained to see the dogs on the other side.

Cautiously, Andrea led the big dogs closer.

•

"Erik, is that you?" Sasha greeted the tiny puppy. Then, with a bit of attitude she added, "Where have you been?"

He seemed to recognize the large white dog. "Sasha . . . is that your name?"

Things were still pretty confusing. The puppy

tried to communicate but he wasn't sure he could make her understand.

"Hurrumph," Sasha exclaimed with disdain. "I'll repeat myself. Where have you been? It was sure no fun for me at first when you left. All they did was cry and carry on. You would think someone died . . . "

A deep shudder went through Sasha. She then said, "I'm sorry Erik. That wasn't nice." Sasha began again. "You see . . . I felt bad too. I missed you. It was lonely."

Trump joined Sasha and began to speak to her.

"That's okay, Sasha," said Trump. "We all deal with death in our own way. Even though I just joined the family, I can tell that Erik and Andrea must have shared an extraordinary friendship. Love never dies, Sasha, and as concerned as I am about the whole situation, this puppy is proof."

"Hmmm." Sasha considered Trump's words and then turned back to the puppy.

"Well Erik, I'm about as happy now as I've ever been. Do you see this handsome Samoyed standing next to me?"

The puppy thought about the question. "Yes – well, I don't know about handsome, but I see another dog. Who is he? Where did he come from?"

Sasha answered the miniature puppy. "That's my

father. His name is Trump. Andrea, Arthur, and I went on a long trip and we found him. They brought him home with us."

"He lives with you? At Arthur and Andrea's?"

"Yes, Erik, he does. And I have never been happier. I always loved Trump, and now he's back with me," Sasha replied confidently.

Then she added, "Are you coming home with us?"

The puppy responded, "I think so. But things are still pretty confusing to me. I can only remember bits and pieces of when I was Andrea's Erik. And now I'm just learning about this Trump . . . "

"Erik?" asked Sasha.

"What?" The puppy was distracted by the news of Trump.

"What was it like to be born?" Sasha asked. "I can't remember."

Trump laughed to himself at Sasha's abrupt change of subject. She was never a particularly deep thinker, but sometimes she came up with good questions.

The puppy replied, "It was weird, really strange. One moment I was part of All That Is and the next moment I found myself in a dark, wet place with my other brothers and sisters. We were very tiny and squirmy, and the space kept getting tighter. One day there was just no more room and my mother," pointing his nose in the direction of White Wolf feeding the other pups, "decided she would let us all come out. And here we are."

"Tell me more," Sasha said.

A puzzled look came over the puppy's face. "I'm tired now Sasha and I'm hungry."

And then, as if his mind went blank, he turned and wobbled back to his mother to resume his dinner.

•

It was time to go. It was hard for Andrea and Arthur to leave their sweet little puppy behind, but they knew he needed to be with his mother a few more weeks before they could bring him home. They bid their farewells to Susan and the downy haired little ones.

As they drove away from Susan's home, Arthur and Andrea decided not to go directly back to Atlanta. Arthur suggested an overnight detour through New Orleans to celebrate Erik's return. Andrea thought it was a great idea. She was high on happiness, knowing her best friend in all the world would soon be home with her. She sat quietly, lost in her thoughts as Arthur drove through the rain. Sasha and Trump slept contentedly.

It seemed it had been nearly an hour since either of them had spoken. Andrea broke the silence. "I'm naming him Amigo," she pronounced to Arthur.

Arthur smiled and asked, "Why would you want to name him that?"

"Because he's my best friend," she responded.

Andrea called Susan right then and asked that she start using his new name. Susan said she would.

CHAPTER THIRTY-SIX

When Andrea and Arthur arrived in New Orleans, it was still raining heavily. In one sense, Andrea was elated at the wonder taking place; however, she felt a vague sadness. She first passed it off as gloomy weather in an unfamiliar city.

The feeling persisted. To her own surprise, that night at dinner, she began to cry over the oysters she had craved on the way to New Orleans. Arthur, usually patient and supportive, was quite puzzled. "Why on earth are you crying when we've just had a miracle?"

"Arthur, I think I finally understand something White Wolf told me in that first dream. He said: 'Erik left the earth as an eagle but must return as a butterfly.' He was trying to caution me that Erik left as my wise, mature teacher and the new puppy would be full of butterfly energy. Eagles are powerful and strong. Butterflies dance with joy and remind us not to take things too seriously."

She continued.

"I think I'm learning yet another lesson. Things don't need to stay the same to be right or good. We grieve for what we lose and then we welcome the new things that come in their place. They never replace, they just add to the richness of our lives. I'll never forget the eagle as I chase my young butterfly."

"So these are learning tears – happy tears?" Arthur asked, a bit relieved.

"Yes, you've got it." Andrea smiled.

Arthur took her hand. "I miss Erik too," Arthur said, "and the new puppy will not change that. Erik's love is back. I knew that today at Susan's. But it will be different. And I have room in my heart for Erik's memory and new adventures with Amigo."

They finished their dinner quietly. On the drive back to the hotel, Andrea and Arthur's conversation was lighter.

Suddenly, Arthur recalled that all their dogs had come to them as adults. "Andrea, Sasha is the only dog we've ever adopted who was close to puppy age, and she was already four months old then. Remember what a terror she was?"

Andrea remembered. The memories of Sasha's destructive chewing wouldn't be erased for a long time. Andrea looked over at Arthur, "You'd better stop at a book store on the way home. I think we're going to need to know a lot more about raising a puppy!"

CHAPTER THIRTY-SEVEN

On December 5, 1998, Andrea, Arthur, Sasha and Trump returned to Florence Morningstar Kennel in Mississippi. They drove in silence much of the trip. Frequently, Arthur glanced over at Andrea, curious at what she was thinking and experiencing. Finally, he asked and she replied, "I'm about to burst with excitement, Arthur! Amigo is eight weeks old and we're finally getting to bring him home!"

Arthur acknowledged her excitement with a bit of trepidation. "Andrea, I'm excited too, but I want you to remember that Erik is coming back to us as a puppy. I just don't want you to get your hopes up that Amigo will remember things the way they were when he was Erik."

"I know, I know, Arthur. I think I'll have more

patience with him reacquainting himself with us than I will when he chews up a pair of my favorite slippers, or worse, a piece of furniture! But it will be wonderful to have him with us again." Andrea dreamily gazed out the window and thought about the life and experiences yet to come with her friend, Amigo. She was as happy as she had been the very first day she met Erik.

Meanwhile, in the back seat, Sasha and Trump were plotting.

•

"I'm afraid the party's over, Sasha," Trump declared. "This is going to be miserable for us. You know that, don't you?"

Sasha replied, "Well, I've not been around puppies before, but I hear they have a lot of energy and sometimes get the other animals in the house in a lot of trouble."

"Oh yes," said Trump. "I remember a beautiful black poodle that I would see sometimes when I was working in the shows. He told me a story about a little Labrador Retriever puppy that came to live with his family. He knocked over the gerbil cage in the child's room and I'm afraid one gerbil – well, let's just say the family no longer had gerbils. Another time, he cornered the family cat and both ended up at the vet with quite a few stitches."

"That doesn't sound so good," Sasha said. "But surely we won't be harmed physically."

"I'll make certain we won't be," Trump responded, baring his teeth. They both giggled.

"I could make his life so miserable he'll want to run away." Sasha responded spitefully.

The two dogs huddled together in the corner of the back seat, scheming.

•

Arriving at the kennel, Andrea barely waited for the car to stop moving before she opened the door and raced to the backyard where she saw all the puppies playing together.

"Amigo! Amigo, come to me little one! I'm here to take you home!" she literally skipped across the yard with excitement.

Amigo heard her voice and looked up from his play. "You're here. You're finally here!" Why did those words seem so familiar as they entered his head?

The puppy's legs had grown stronger and his run was deliberate and effortless as he dashed across the grass to Andrea. She quickly noticed that he had grown in just four short weeks and even though he was still covered in baby fur, her puppy was healthy and happy.

As Andrea and Arthur said their good-byes to Susan, Amigo made the rounds to his mother and brothers and sisters. "Be a good dog, Amigo," his mother instructed. "You won't understand this yet, but you and Andrea have much to do together. And she and Arthur will be loving parents to you. I will see you again one day, my little son."

And with that farewell, White Wolf nudged her son's nose, gave him final loving licks across his face, then turned and walked away.

Amigo sat in Andrea's lap most of the long ride back to Atlanta. The excitement of his adventure heading home, the odd feeling he had about leaving his birth family, and several hours without a nap soon induced him to shut his eyes. He snuggled into a ball and felt very safe with his mom, whose fingers were gently combing through his fur.

"I'm going to love my new life," Amigo thought, and sleep pulled his eyelids closed.

As the puppy drifted into a dream state, a familiar voice rang in his head. He sensed deep love. "Your new journey has begun, young friend. Never fear, as I will be close by to guide and protect you."

"Thank you, White Wolf," Amigo expressed silently. Then, he slept deeply.

Andrea dozed as well, waking as Arthur navigated the rough I-20 pavement. By now she was accustomed to and comforted by the frequent musical messages she received, so it was not a surprise when she woke to Rod Stewart's raspy rendition of Van Morrison's "Have I told You Lately That I Love You?" Those lyrics, more like a prayer than a song, became Andrea's prayer of gratitude. She thought about how much territory she had covered in her heart in a short period. From grief sprang hope, and now . . . joy seemed possible once again.

•

In the backseat, trouble was escalating. "Look at him all settled in her lap like he owns her! Who does he think he is?" Sasha jealously remarked to Trump.

"Well, as I mentioned on the first trip to Mississippi, she believes he's her old Erik. And while I never knew him, he must have been pretty special for him to come back. You may as well get used to it, Sasha. He's here to stay. I was just kidding when I growled a while ago." Then he hesitated and added,

"Maybe."

"He may be back, but he's not the same as Erik. He's a puppy who's going to take a lot of their time – which means attention away from us. I just don't like it."

"Oh, dear daughter, what you don't like is not being number one anymore! Be careful or you'll find yourself slipping even more out of favor."

Sasha responded with one of her nastiest huffs and retreated to the far corner of the car. Trump soon joined her, because that's what they did – they were together in everything.

Glancing into the rear view mirror, it was obvious to Arthur that Trump and Sasha were united in their contempt of Amigo. The two dogs sat side by side staring out the back window. Their lives were changed forever and they seemed to know it. Arthur remarked to Andrea, "Trump and Sasha are partners in distress over the new puppy. I sure hope we don't have trouble brewing."

"Oh, they'll be fine," Andrea said, dismissing his concerns. Little did she know the antics that awaited.

CHAPTER THIRTY-EIGHT

Amigo's first year was filled with joyful fun, harrowing fights with the big dogs Trump and Sasha, as well as a few minor runaway adventures. Fortunately all near-disasters ended well.

Since the Sedona trip just after Erik's death, Andrea and Arthur had been discussing a move back to Arizona. As Amigo's one-year birthday passed, they thought the timing was right to make a reconnaissance trip to check out the real estate market there. Things were relatively quiet. It had been some time since any of the dogs had needed stitches after an ugly fight, and the three seemed to have worked out their pack order and rules. A cross-country trip seemed possible.

Plans were made for Arthur to drive out to Phoenix with the three dogs. Andrea would fly in and join them, and the family would stay for a month of house-hunting and much needed vacation.

Arthur enjoyed long drives. Andrea disliked them. So they decided that Arthur would leave for Phoenix on Monday morning of Thanksgiving week while Andrea was on a business trip in Cincinnati. She would return to Atlanta for a one-day client meeting and then fly out to Phoenix to join Arthur and the dogs on Thanksgiving Day.

Arthur planned to stay the first night of his trip in Baton Rouge, LA. He made his way there without any trouble, arriving just as night fell. He decided to overnight at a dog-friendly La Quinta Inn just off Interstate 10. This would make for easy access the next morning as he continued on the three day trip to Phoenix. The plan made sense.

About 7 p.m., Arthur pulled into the La Quinta, parked in front of the entrance and left the dogs in the car. He could see them peering out the windows as he checked in at the front desk. The clerk was cheerful and made him feel at home after a long drive. She gave him a key to room 109, a first-floor location next to the parking lot. Arthur drove around to the room, unlocked the door and led the dogs into their home for the night. Bowls of fresh food and water helped them settle into the room.

No more than a few minutes later, the door

unexpectedly opened. The man standing there immediately recognized the mistake – and unfortunately, so did Amigo. The hotel clerk who had been so nice had accidentally checked someone else into Arthur's room!

Amigo was tired of being confined during the long ride with Sasha and Trump and was ready to expend some pent-up energy. Without a second thought, he took advantage of the opportunity. Amigo bolted past Arthur and headed out into the darkness. The surprised man standing in the doorway covered his mouth with his hands. Arthur followed Amigo, frantic with thoughts of disaster.

The inn was located right beside the Interstate 10 freeway. On one side of the building was a busy gas station and on the other, the first of many restaurants. All provided enormous opportunities for exploration. Moving cars, trucks, and motorcycles crowded the pavement. Amigo was nowhere to be seen.

Amigo had retained one of Erik's less endearing qualities: that of reckless runaway. Arthur knew that he was going have trouble finding the dog and panic gripped him.

Immediately and with dread, Arthur called Andrea's cell phone. She was in the Cincinnati airport waiting to board a plane back to Atlanta. She listened as Arthur cried, "That poor little puppy. He'll be lost. He doesn't know what to do; he's just a puppy. And the freeway! Oh, I can't believe this has happened!"

Andrea couldn't believe what she was hearing. She felt a pang of fear deep within her midsection and for a moment she froze, feeling her mouth dry up so that the words would not come. Then, all of a sudden she kicked into gear. Very calmly, yet deliberately, she told Arthur what to do.

"Go out and enlist everyone you can find to help capture Amigo. People who love their own pets will want to help. Assemble a crew: people pumping gas, workers who may be able to leave their posts. Ask the desk clerk to help you. Get as many as you can, then get Sasha and Trump in the car so that if Amigo comes back, he'll see them. Do it now, quickly! And Arthur . . . " she spoke softly and with resolve, "we will find him. He'll be fine."

Andrea hung up the phone and noticed that while her body was visibly trembling, she had an inner calm. "Yes," she thought to herself. "He will be okay. I know this; I don't know how I know – but I am certain of it."

•

"Princess, come join me," White Wolf called to the Princess, who was fast becoming his apprentice.

"There's a drama unfolding with the young one, Amigo. He's giving his family some trouble. Have a look."

The Princess peered through the veil and gasped just as Amigo narrowly skirted a pickup truck leaving the gas station. "Oh, White Wolf, he's in real danger! What an incorrigible puppy. He seems to have no fear. He's in danger out there alone. You've got to help him!"

"Yes, Princess. I can warn him of the danger, but he might not listen. Amigo is confident and bold, but young and foolhardy too. I can provide guidance, but he has free will. Even though he knows that Andrea adores him and would be devastated if anything happened to him, he's not afraid of anything – not even death."

White Wolf continued, "It seems that Andrea has done what's needed this time, but Amigo's a different story. I'll speak to Amigo and coax him back to the car. I'm proud of Andrea though. She just passed a very big test – one of many."

"A test? What do you mean?" the Princess mused, more to herself than to White Wolf.

•

Methodically, as if checking off a to-do list, Andrea approached the Delta Airlines ticket counter and spoke calmly, yet rapidly. "I was about to leave for Atlanta, but my husband just lost our son outside a hotel room in Baton Rouge. I need to get there."

The agent didn't speak or make eye contact but began typing rapidly. Andrea prayed silently as the woman typed. After a minute that felt like an eternity, the agent looked up at Andrea and handed her a boarding pass. "There's a flight leaving in twenty minutes. You can make it if you go quickly to the other end of the concourse. Good luck."

Andrea thanked her and began running, heart pounding. She got to the gate as the last few passengers were boarding and joined the line, trying to catch her breath.

•

Meanwhile, in Baton Rouge, Arthur had assembled a sizeable search party that included guests just arriving at La Quinta. He pleaded with the gas station attendant to help him find his dog. A person pumping gas said she would help as well.

As Arthur hurriedly put Sasha and Trump in the car, he thought of how ironic it was to be looking for Amigo on the same interstate that Erik had used for one of his escapes many years before, in another part of the country.

Arthur briefed his crew of helpers; then set out himself. Soon a swarm of people were rushing everywhere in search of the bolt of white fur on lightning-fast legs.

Arthur searched up and down the access road praying Amigo wouldn't venture onto the dangerous interstate. No sign of him anywhere! In desperation, he returned to the hotel parking lot hoping Amigo was exploring closer by.

But Amigo's curiosity had led him away from the hotel and toward a heavily wooded area about a half mile away. He had moved swiftly across the open ground near the hotel and restaurants, where pavement and manicured lawns made his path clear.

Initially his destination had been a field of brush that seemed to separate the commercial area from the woods, but as soon as he entered the field, an explosion of provocative scents bombarded his nose. There were so many new earth smells and animal odors that he felt himself being pulled in a hundred directions at once. Frantically, he began to follow each lead.

Driven by the frenzy of smells, Amigo pressed on, farther and farther across the field of tangled bushes and tall grasses toward the dark woods. He was oblivious to those searching for him and completely unaware of the potential danger lurking ahead.

·

White Wolf had watched over Amigo constantly during that first year and was always prepared to intervene at a time of crisis. Amigo had a job to do and one poor choice could endanger his life and threaten his path of friendship and learning with Andrea. It was time to step in.

Softly at first, Amigo heard the voice in his head: "Amigo, this is your friend, White Wolf. I'm here to help you. You have much to do with this woman, Andrea, and you must not get hurt. Allow yourself to be found."

"Whoa! What was that?!" The voice jarred Amigo. "Who's in my head?"

White Wolf responded more clearly and firmly, "I am your guardian angel, Amigo. I am White Wolf and I am with you at all times. Hear me. You must return to Arthur. Allow yourself to be found by these people searching for you. Do it now."

Amigo replied to the strange voice, "Look, I don't know who you are or how you got in my head, but this adventure is great fun. I want to explore some more. Thank you, but I'll be fine."

"Amigo, you are mortal," White Wolf continued, "If you had an accident, Andrea and Arthur would be very, very sad. Don't do this."

Hearing voices in his head was a totally new experience for Amigo, yet there was a subtle familiarity. He remembered the voice. "This feels creepy," he thought. He continued walking slowly with no particular direction in mind, concentrating on the message he had just received.

A few minutes later, Amigo looked up. He was at the edge of the woods and tall pine trees beckoned him to enter. Amigo crossed the tree line. Once inside the forest, his footpath became easier due to a heavy pine needle carpet which forbids the growth of the area's thorny vines and bushes. With the terrain more maneuverable, he allowed his nose and ears to guide the way.

The sound of rushing water coaxed him to a narrow but deep stream fed by runoff water. Recent rains had not only provided a heavy flow, but also softened the dirt along the steep bank.

"A drink of water would be good," Amigo thought

as he looked down at the stream. He eased himself over the edge, carefully placing each front paw to test the earth for slipperiness. He proceeded – so far, so good. Then, about half-way down the bank Amigo began to slide down, down, down.

"I don't dare move. I'll make it worse." Amigo sensed futility as his back legs moved uncontrollably toward his front legs, resulting in a cold, wet slide down the bank. Fortunately a small tree broke his downward movement and allowed him to come to rest on a small ledge.

"What a predicament! I'm glad Trump and Sasha aren't here to see this!" Amigo thought humbly. "Now, how will I get out of here?"

He didn't have much time to think about a solution. Above the noise of the water came the strange howling and yipping sounds of several animals nearby. Too close. The sounds seemed to be moving toward him.

"What was it that White Wolf character said? 'Danger?' Did he say I'm 'in danger'?" Amigo felt a pang of panic.

The sounds were coming from a pack of wild dogs that lived in the woods and fed from the restaurant dumpsters along the access road. Their keen senses of smell had picked up Amigo's presence on their turf.

•

"Look, White Wolf, look! You've got to help him out of harm's way. Can't you make him listen to you?" The Princess pleaded to her mentor.

White Wolf replied, "I've got to get through to him. Now. Clearly this young one doesn't have the street sense to defend himself against a bunch of wild dogs. Erik might have had a fighting chance, but I can't risk it with this inexperienced puppy."

White Wolf took a deep breath and chose his words carefully: "Amigo, pay attention! There is time for me to say this only once. You are in immediate danger! Do you hear that howling and barking just beyond you? It's coming from a pack of vicious wild dogs who've picked up your scent. They're not happy you're prowling through their territory. You must get out of these woods and back to safety. Now move it before it's too late!"

Amigo got the message! He could sense the animals coming closer but there was another problem.

It was impossible to go back up the slippery bank. The only way was down, and it might mean landing in the stream. He forced his body to relax and his front legs led the way as he began sliding downward once again. As he approached the water's edge, the slope flattened out just enough to allow him to get all four feet beneath his body. He quickly dug in and raced along the stream looking for an area where the bank's slope would allow him to climb out. "I've got to get back up to the top. I'm a 'sitting duck' trapped in this ravine," Amigo thought.

A short distance ahead, the grade of the bank became slightly less steep. Entangled roots were embedded in the soil. That would help. Up he struggled against the loose dirt, finally grabbing purchase on the grass at the top.

The sounds from the dogs were dangerously close now. Amigo couldn't tell which side of the creek they were on. Somehow he knew it wouldn't matter. They would know the fastest way across. That fact, and the voice that had come to him moments earlier in his head, kept his attention.

At the rim of the bank, Amigo quickly checked his bearings and dashed in the direction from which he had come. At least, he hoped it was the same direction.

He remembered that the trees had been taller and less dense along the edge of the woods and their canopy had permitted rays of moonlight to penetrate the darkness. It was still very dark where he was. He had to keep pushing forward as the wild animals were closing in, encouraging his every step. The bramble field that marked the end of the woods had to be coming up soon.

"Moonlight up ahead through the tree tops! Go, go, go!" Amigo was talking to himself now. It was a beautiful sight but Amigo knew the hardest part was ahead of him – the trip through the underbrush.

Leaving the forest behind, he thrust himself into the thick tangle of bushes and thorns, realizing it would slow him down. It was the only way out he knew. The stickers latched into his fur as he struggled through them, drawing pain as they pricked the skin. He slowed to try to find a better way around them.

Encouragingly, White Wolf spoke, "Keep moving, Amigo. You've got to get out of the underbrush. They know the terrain better than you and will trap you if you're in there too long. Follow the sound of my voice and I will lead you out."

Instinctively, Amigo finally trusted the voice that seemed to be just in front of him. He fought to keep up with the speed required and now fully understood his life depended upon doing so.

The dogs were so close he could hear their bodies snapping the dried grasses behind him. They weren't slowed at all by the prickly bushes. He focused. "Just a little bit farther," he told himself. "It seems to be clearing ahead."

"I'll get you out, Amigo. Just stay with me. Follow my voice. You're almost out of the brush and into a clearing where you can run fast."

Amigo's breath was coming in rapid pants now. In order to make a break for it as soon as he hit the clearing, he knew he had to somehow get a second wind. On the other side of the brush, the hotel parking lot was at least two hundred yards away. He would have to fly to put some distance between himself and the pack.

As he broke free of the brush, his legs began to move so rapidly they barely touched the ground. It was as if something lifted him and made the running effortless. He could hear human voices in the distance. A familiar male voice was calling: "Amigo?"

As Amigo moved toward the sound of Arthur's voice, he humbly expressed gratitude. "Thank you, White Wolf."

REFLECTIONS

As the harrowing adventure in Baton Rouge began, White Wolf told the Princess that Andrea had just passed a very big test. And, she passed it before Amigo was out of harm's way.

What Andrea did that evening was remarkable, especially given that her precious Amigo, her miracle, was in grave danger. Simply, she surrendered to the matter at hand, the ordeal, yet she didn't let her fear replace her faith.

Fear is one of the most dangerous of human emotions. Its presence can cause the very things humans are afraid of to manifest before their eyes. When Arthur called Andrea and told her Amigo was lost, she could have panicked. She could have allowed her feelings of anger and despair to overwhelm her, or she could have become cynical, thinking that nothing good ever lasts. She could have crawled back into her shell. But instead, faith and love – the two things that Erik had taught Andrea – prevailed. Oh sure, she was agitated and her heart was racing as she moved through the airport making plans to go to Baton Rouge. The adrenaline rush produced all of the typical symptoms of anxiety. But this human condition, this emotional state, had a partner.

As the call from Arthur filled her conscious mind, Andrea instantly began to pray. And for perhaps the first time ever, she consciously experienced the profound responsibility that accompanies prayer.

Prayer is a conversation between the part of us that is human and the part of us that is God. At first, when Andrea reached out from her heart and mind pleading for a miracle, begging for intercession, she felt an immense aloneness. Her faith was tested in that moment as she realized this was not an appeal to a man in the sky. It was not simply a one-way request delivered to an outside party. It required tuning into the love and light of All That Is. The conduit that had been restored by the experience with Erik's life, death, and rebirth of Amigo was open and functioning.

When Andrea tuned in, she felt that Amigo was safe and protected. But her responsibility did not stop there. Her strong emotions served as catalysts for action in alignment with light and love. Andrea had to take action – that's what humans do. Her actions that evening were governed by a knowing in her heart that all would work out.

Prayer is an experience of faith and trust that love and light will eventually and always prevail. It transmutes negative emotions, freeing us to tune in to purpose-driven guidance. This does not mean it will always turn out the way our human mind thinks it should. But there are no Divine mistakes.

Arthur called Andrea to tell her Amigo had been found just before she boarded the plane to Baton Rouge. Pushing her luck, she rapidly explained to the ticket agent that her son, who had been lost in Baton Rouge, was now found. She told him that she now needed to be on that last flight to Atlanta for a business meeting in the morning.

Once again, Andrea was successful in her efforts to make it back to the opposite end of the concourse and was able to get on the Atlanta flight. Taking her original first-class seat, she became aware that her heart was pounding wildly in her chest. As she tried to calm down physically, she recalled the strange sequence of events that had just occurred. She was reminded of the Russian proverb: "Pray to God but row for shore." She smiled at the thought and exhaled, releasing the deepest breath of her life.

"The human emotional system can be broken down into roughly two elements: fear and love. Love is of the soul. Fear is of the personality."

Gary Zukav

"Seat of the Soul"

A Preview of Book Two

Several years later . . .

Amigo was in a foul mood given that it was August and outdoor time was seriously limited in the hot desert of Arizona. Arthur had been a bit down in the dumps, too – at least until this morning.

"They're rushing around like their hair's on fire. You'd think they were preparing for royalty," Amigo said to Sasha, waking her from a deep sleep.

"Nothing would surprise me," Sasha replied, then returned to her nap.

Amigo resigned himself to a nap as well and he didn't awaken until he heard Andrea and Arthur come through the front door. "What in the ____?" Amigo couldn't believe his eyes!

Arthur was holding a puppy! As Arthur approached Amigo, his initial indignation turned to shock, then excitement.

"Could it be? Princess, is that you?"

ACKNOWLEDGMENTS

ANDREA

A 13-year labor of love, Erik's Hope is more a mission to me than a project. So many people share in the realization of this mission, it is impossible to acknowledge all of you here. You are each in my heart.

To everyone who knew and loved Erik, and who grieved with me – you are part of the miracle. Alice Barz, Beth Ballmann, Barbara Ford, Sandy Keefe, Art Parfitt, Linda Tennant, Tanya Uherka – you all were there when I didn't even realize how much I needed you. I am especially grateful to Dr. Pat Zook, for your wise counsel throughout Erik's life and beyond, and for your belief in me and the gift this story is for others. A very special thank you to Susan Boyd, Amigo's midwife, for boldly expressing what you knew to be true, and for literally delivering a miracle. Thank you,

Erin Michael, for guiding my way to Susan.

Thank you to Becky Didier, for acting as producer of the early version of this story. I don't know if the story would have ever been told without your persuasion and help.

So many encouraged this project by providing feedback or simply just believing in it. In the early days, my conversations with Nancy Beauregard, Jakki Brooks, Karla Boyd, Judy Goodman, Kris Haley and Deborah Waitley influenced my resolve to share the story, even as I seemingly procrastinated. Later, as the manuscript came alive, I was blessed with generous friends who volunteered candid advice. I realized through your feedback that I had to live the journey before I could put it to paper. Later, I had to be brave enough to write the story that I had lived. I am so grateful to Susan Reece for tireless encouragement and support, and especially for coaxing White Wolf into existence. Thank you DeAnna Burton, for helping me understand firsthand the power of the message, and for opening your heart to me.

A warm thank you to friends and clients who enthusiastically reviewed the manuscript and gave valuable direction for positioning the work: Dita Couch, Tammy Dowd, Suzanne Ficquette, Tracy Freeman, Shelby Horner, Jeanette Irwin, Debbie

Johnstone, Don Karell, Glenda Knebel, Pam McIntosh, Lynne Ramsey, Alex Seelbach, Jan Taylor, Krisie Warner, Paty Williams, Susanne Wilson, and my dear wine cl . . . *err* . . . book club sisters, Dianne Aguilar, Deb Rauen, Dee Robbins, Joette Schmidt, and Dr. Kit Slocum.

Thank you to Brenda Seelbach for tirelessly managing the many directions this project took, and for lending your keen editorial eye.

To Sheppard Lake: thank you for always reminding me of my purpose here.

Of course I am forever grateful to my dear friend, Sara Burden, for helping tell the story and for listening as I laughed and cried through the memories. In doing so, you helped illuminate the lessons learned so others can benefit.

To my sweet husband Arthur: you show me as close to unconditional love as a human can manage. I know you share in my gratitude to all who are mentioned here, as well as to the four-leggeds that bless our life together.

Finally, I want to personally thank everyone who played a part in Amigo's life and helped me through his recent loss. The specifics will have to wait for the next story, when it's Amigo's turn to teach.

ACKNOWLEDGMENTS

SARA

They say "it takes a village." That's not true; it takes more than that! My appreciation goes to the "country" that supported us throughout the building of the book and getting the message to the public:

My family – Lee, Pat, Hunter, Madison Hill, and Wes, Rachel, Race Burden.

Friends who gave their time to read the manuscript and provide comments and support: Renee Van Aeist-Bouma, Jackson Hanks, Marjean Henderson, Ann King, Tom Long, Chet Walden, Vida Walden and many others.

My wonderful sisterhood here in Atlanta – "Southern Ladies up to Something" who not only critiqued the material but remained fiercely enthusiastic about the success of Erik's Hope: Caroline Calder, Chris Bosonetto-Doane, Cecilia Roach, Deborah Latham, Essie Escobedo, Jan Martinez,

Linda Zuk, Ria Bruns, Sandra Britt, Sherry Wheat.

And a very special thanks to Andrea Chilcote, who entrusted me with her extraordinary story and the beautiful animal spirits of Erik and Amigo, without whom this could not have been told.

Thank you to our agent, Devra Jacobs of Dancing Word Group, who freed us to tell the whole story, making it what it is today, and to Maria Brunner, for sharing the vision. Thank you to David Culp for the awesome photography that captures the essence of the work.

ANDREA CHILCOTE

Andrea Chilcote is Erik's person, the woman who experienced and documented Erik's real life love, loss and rebirth. She credits much of her work today to the lessons received from her teacher, Erik.

Andrea is an author, executive coach, and leadership development expert. She brings to the reader current practical knowledge of the issues and concerns people are facing at this difficult time. She has a keen skilled and intuitive ability to facilitate transformational change in individuals, and her writing offers this opportunity to the reader.

Andrea has authored numerous personal development articles and programs, and designs and delivers leadership curriculum for diverse businesses through her consulting practice, Morningstar Ventures. Andrea lives in Cave Creek, Arizona with her husband, dogs and horses.

SARA BURDEN

Sara Burden added fantasy and adventure to Erik and Andrea's true-life story. Equipped with creative imagination and her love for the Chilcote canine family, she helped bring the characters to life. When Andrea asked Sara to collaborate in the writing of Erik's Hope, she was delighted to do so.

As Vice President of Walden Businesses, a prominent southeastern mergers and acquisitions firm, Sara is featured speaker on numerous talk radio shows and conducts accounting and law firm seminars and workshops. She has addressed women's professional business groups and has taught educational classes at international conferences for the mergers and acquisitions industry. Sara lives in Atlanta, Georgia.